House of Sand

Ron Saint

House of Sand

Copyright © 2016 Ron Saint

Published by Jakers Publishing, Roswell, GA.

Cover by Eric Fournier

ISBN: 0997498706
ISBN-13: 9780997498707

DEDICATION

In Memory of

My brother, William (Bill Ed), who loved and lived a
stimulating life and my sister, Mary Elizabeth.

ACKNOWLEDGMENTS

I want to thank

Mike Kennedy, Author of, Gender Specific.
Georgia Kraft, Author of, Fireflies in a Jar.
Bill Gibson, Playwright and Author of, Coming and Going.
Kim Muller is working on her, Supernatural Thriller.

A special thanks to my editor, Emily Thrasher, who spent a lot of time with this book.

PROLOGUE

Fifteen minutes after the last explosive was set in place, the camp's ammo and fuel supplies were giant fireballs. The team had only a few minutes to go in and extract what they referred to as "packages". Joseph Defoe and his wife, Martha, millionaire owners of Defoe Toy Distributing had been in the company of a group of rebels for one week before the team had been notified telling them Joseph's son had received a ransom note demanding two million dollars.

For this team to be on the mission meant the family had connections with some high-ups in Washington. Usually, for the team to be requested meant there was strong probability, after the money was paid Joseph and Martha would be killed. They have never failed on a mission, and they came with a high price tag.

Fire shot into the sky as the four men made their way into the camp from different directions. After an intense twenty-minute firefight, they had what they came for and were out of the camp. Half their work had been accomplished. They still had to get the packages home safely.

The pilot saw the flare trail upward. He started the engine, and the rotors went into motion, slowly at first, picking up speed with each rotation. In no time, he was airborne moving toward his team members.

When he was over the place, he saw a signal letting him know the team was in the clear. He maneuvered the chopper into position and M-60 rounds pierced every tent in the camp. It wasn't long before the firing stopped. Another signal and the Huey sat down and made an extraction.

CHAPTER 1

July 4th weekend 1974

Robert Ludlow and his wife Jennie, along with their twelve-year-old son were enjoying a relaxing day on the beach in Panama City Beach. A few days before, they had been sailing on the Florida coast aboard their thirty-foot Tartan.

Two miles up the beach from their hotel, Robert finished the first leg of his jogging, turned and headed back. There were plenty of bikini clad babes to catch a man's eye, but the only woman who could get his motor running at the speed he liked was waiting back where he had started his run.

Jennie lay on a towel in a bikini, showing off her golden tanned flat stomach while waiting for Robert. Her long blonde hair pinned on top of her head. At five-foot-nine she had long legs capable of competing with any model. Jennie turned on her side and braced herself on one elbow and watched their soon-to-be teenage son dive into the waves and come back up shaking the saltwater off his face.

Robert ended his run, slipped his shoes off and looked down at his wife lying on her stomach, her arms folded under her face. She had the strap to her top unfastened, so she did not cut her tan in half. His eyes traced her long body from head to toe, stopping halfway down. She sensed his presence and moved her ass slowly a few times.

Robert's motor revved as he thought, You hussy. If we didn't have Chris with us, I'd have you in our room in two minutes. He always had those thoughts when she teased him, which she did at every opportunity. He forced his eyes away from Jennie and scanned the water. There you are. He saw Chris standing on the surf. Robert walked to the edge of the water and waved to his son but got no response. Chris was looking back at the wave about to take him on a voyage. At the right time he jumped and landed face down on the tube. Robert waited for the wave to place his son and the tube at his feet.

Chris stood. "Wow, did you see me, Dad?"

"I saw it all. Let's go back out." Robert ran toward a wave and dived into it. He surfaced, turned and waved at Jennie, who was now sitting up facing the water, then he yelled for Chris to, "Come on."

The two-mile run and the half hour of playing in the ocean had done away with Robert's breakfast. "I'm ready to eat something, how about you?"

"Can I play a little longer?"

He ruffled his son's hair. "Don't go out too far. I'm going to talk to your mother."

Robert plopped down on the sand next to his wife who was on now her back wearing sunglasses. Her bathing suit top lay over her breasts with the straps still unfastened. He put a finger under her breasts, careful not to disturb the unsecured garment, and zigzagged his finger across her body down to the top of her suit bottom.

"Watch it, big boy," she said.

"I am watching. As a matter of fact, I can't take my eyes off you."

"It's good we have a two-bedroom condo."

Chris came dragging the tube across the sand. "I'm ready to turn this thing in and go eat."

Robert parked in the lot at Captain Anderson's Restaurant, shut the engine off and turned to his passengers. "Let's go put our name in for a table. Then we'll go see what the fishing boats brought in. I think they're arriving now."

Excited Chris blurted out, "Oh, boy, I hope they got some big ones."

They reached the slips as a few of the boats were unloading their catch of the day. Someone had hooked a large Cobia and had it hanging from a hook, the tail touching the dock.

Chris walked next the fish and turned to his parents, "Look, I'll bet it weighs fifty pounds."

It was as long as his son, who was five feet. Robert figured about a pound an inch. "Every bit and more, about sixty pounds I'll bet."

"What time is the potential, or is he a customer, meeting us?" Jennie said.

"I've bagged this one already. The papers are drawn up; he's going to sign them tomorrow. It's a good thing, too, because I need this contract so I can get the loan from the bank. He and his wife should be here in about thirty minutes."

"Way to go, my Bobby."

Friday, December 13th 1974

"I told you; we don't want to do this anymore. So, what will it take to get you out of our lives?"

"Come now, Jeffrey. Or should I call you Jeff?"

"I would prefer you didn't call me anything. Forget you ever knew my wife and me."

"Now, Jeff. Is this how you are going to thank me for the loan."

"I've paid you back, now will you please forget about us."

"I'm afraid I can't. Not after introducing you to my associates, so Jeff, with the two of you knowing so much, I only see one way we could stop doing business."

"This was your intention all along, wasn't it? Sucking us in and never letting us out. Well, I'm saying it. We are finished with you."

"You have noticed I'm paying you for each trip you make for me now." The overweight, chubby faced Lesmeck looked at Jeffrey's wife. "Are you ready to give up the lifestyle the money affords you?"

Jefferey's wife, Mary, used an open hand to push air at the man. "Yes, I'm more than ready."

Jeffrey raised a finger. "You bringing your friends to our house and them put their hands on my wife was more than we care to live with. So, we are through." Jeffrey pointed at the door. "Bye."

The big man walked to the door and turned back. "I hope you know what you are doing."

"Oh, I know exactly what I'm doing, getting as far away from you as we can."

Lesmeck opened the door, but instead of

leaving he motioned for someone, and two men appeared. "Meet my associates." Lesmeck backed away from the door and the two men walked in; one was much taller than the other and dressed in a yellow suit. The other wore a brown suit.

"Hey, what is this? I don't want those guys in my home," Jeffrey said.

"You said you wanted to dissolve our partnership, didn't you, Jeff? Well, the only way I see fit to do so is to let Jay and Martin take care of it. Y'all know what today's date is. I believe there might be something to this Friday the thirteenth thing. Help yourselves to whatever, guys. I'll be in the van." The big man shook his head and said, "Such a lovely couple too." He could hear Jeff and Mary pleading as he closed the door.

CHAPTER 2

Monday, December 16th 1974, Buckhead (Atlanta, GA)

Roy Cobb leaned back in his chair and placed his hands behind his head, pleased with the contract he had signed. Getting a loan at half the bank's interest rate was a blessing. Besides, he was almost over-extended on his credit. With the loan came a new account moving freight out of Miami at full tariff price, with the first shipment starting today. And the customer picking it up from his dock in Atlanta was too sweet to be true.

Tuesday, December 17th 1974

Robert Ludlow walked into his business on Monday morning and was shocked. He could not believe what he saw, or didn't see. What he didn't see was more than half of his sewing machines. He stood, dumbfounded, as he scanned the room. The back roll-up door was open, and the wall was visible. Because the material used for making pants his company sells was gone, boxes of thread, cloth, everything. He sat down in the nearest chair and put his head in his hands. How could this have happened? The alarm.

Heart pounding, he rushed to the box on the wall thinking. Why didn't you call the police and tell them there was a break-in, get the hell here, now. Not in those exact words, but you should have called. The wires had been cut, and the box was on the floor. What the hell. Robert did what the box should have done, called the cops.

The cops had finished their report and were leaving. Robert leaned on the door frame, looking into the large room where everything goes on making his company work. Nothing was happening now. A foot scraped across the tile floor behind him followed by a monotone voice.

"I saw the police leaving as I came up. What happened, Robert?"

Dazed Robert didn't move. "Come over here and have a look."

Lesmeck moved next to Robert. "Am I looking for something?"

"Tell me. What do you see?"

"I don't see very much. You seem to be missing some of your equipment."

"And my entire inventory."

"How terrible."

"I'll be out of business if I can't secure a loan to replace the stuff."

"Well, how do you stand with the bank?"

"I'm in good standing, but I'm tapped out with them."

"I think it's time for us to have a talk."

Jennie was aware of the bad news. With dinner out of the way and Chris in bed, Robert delivered the good news to his wife.

.   "You mean he offered to loan you some money?"

"Yes, and you won't believe the interest rate." He stared at his grinning wife.

After a moment, she said, "Well, I might if you tell me." She eased a cup to her lips. "Who is this, guy?" She sipped from the cup.

"His name is Lesmeck. He came in a few weeks ago while looking for a building to lease. He's been back a few times, and we've had a few conversations. The only thing I have to do is go to New York and meet with his associates."

Jennie held the cup a few inches from her mouth. "When will you be going?"

"I'll leave Tomorrow morning and come back in the evening."

"Kind of sudden, isn't it? But if you think he's okay, I guess you did the right thing."

"Not only was it the right thing, but it was also my only option." With it settled Robert held his arms out as a signal for Jennie to take a seat on his lap. "Come here you sexy thing."

Wednesday, December 18th 1974

Jennie waited for Robert to open the door before she eased herself out of the driver's seat and slid over the console to the passenger seat. Her legs were apart, revealing she wasn't wearing underwear. She liked flashing Robert when they were in places like this and all he could do was look. It gave her a feeling a racecar driver gets when he fires up the engine. You know it will give you a fast and forceful ride all the way across the finish line. She always remained expressionless and without acknowledgment she did it. Robert knew when and where to look for those flashes.

She leaned over and kissed him long on the lips, darting her tongue in and out a couple of times, then backed away, subtly sliding her hand across his crotch and adjusted herself in the seat. "I thought you were coming back this evening."

"Yeah, me too," he said

"How was the trip?"

"Weird is all I can say. I'll tell you about it on the drive home."

Her head was resting on the headrest, turned in his direction. "No. I come first. I don't want any distractions."

It didn't sound strong enough to be a demand. Robert knew it wasn't a question. It was a request. Whatever it was, there was only one way to answer it. Robert smiled, leaned over, put a hand on her face and kissed her. "To hell with my trip, let's break the speed limit getting home."

Two hours after they walked through the door, Jennie felt not only did she have a strong finish, but she was waved across the finish line with the checkered flag and brought home the trophy. Robert was on his side taking in her lovely body. Jennie was raised on one elbow with a hand on his chest.

"Tell me about your trip," she said.

Robert puckered his lips for a moment. "Those associates of his were a little, what can I say? Odd, is what they are."

"What do you mean?"

"Before I left, Lesmeck handed me a briefcase with instructions do not open it. He told me to give it to the bigger guy of the two."

"Papers for the loan, I guess," Jenni said.

"I thought so, too, but it had a strap around the middle with a lock on it in addition to the hasp locks. Lesmeck told me again not to open it. Only this time he said, 'under no circumstances are you to open the case.'"

Jennie screwed her lips into a pucker. "Overcautious I'd say, but does it make them odd?"

"No, but they were definitely kind of off the rail."

"So, where was their office?"

"Even more bizarre. I didn't leave the airport."

"I guess all they wanted were the papers, and maybe they were busy."

"I guess you could be right. When I gave them the case, they handed me a small suitcase and told me, 'Don't open it.' Then they turned and walked away. Lesmeck met me when I disembarked the plane, took the suitcase and said he would see me next time."

"What did he mean?"

"The next time he comes by the plant, I guess. Anyway, I told him we were going out of town for the rest of the Christmas school break."

CHAPTER 3

Sunday, December 22nd 1974

Lesmeck, Corso, five-ten 200 pounds, and three other men were ready to take seats at a table. Milo Gulchie, the head of the operation from New York, Alfonso Ruden ran operations in Miami and Fidel Lopez from South America. On the table in front of each man was a glass of fine wine; behind each man stood two bodyguards, each had brought.

"Gentlemen," Gulchie said. "I propose a toast."

Each lifted their glass of wine and held it in the air, waiting for the toast to be announced.

Gulchie nodded to each man. "To our new beginning!"

The men drank from their glasses.

When they lowered their glasses, one man behind three of the big shots pulled their chairs out and they took a seat.

Lesmeck, still standing, looked at the shorter of the two men behind him. "Martin my chair."

Martin glanced at the chair, then at Lesmeck. "What, Boss?"

"My chair."

"What about your chair."

"Martin, would you please pull my chair out so

I can sit down."

"Me? What's the matter with you?"

"Would you please do as I ask?"

Jay grabbed the chair. "I got it, Boss."

Lesmeck took his seat. "You two may go."

The eight men headed toward the living room.

"Did the boss hurt his arm?" Martin said. "Why did he ask me to pull his chair out?"

"Don't worry about it, and come on, shit-for-brains," Jay said.

In the living room, Gulchie's and Lopez's bodyguards were taking turns punching each other in their stomachs to see who could make the other concede. Lesmeck's and Ruden's men were outclassed and had no desire to be human punching bags.

"Why did you guys pull your bosses chair out for them?" Martin asked.

"He don't know nothing, guys," Jay said. "They call it being a man's man."

One of Gulchie's men spoke up, "It's called a gentleman's gentleman. But we're not. We serve as a valet as well as their bodyguards."

"A valet? Guys who park cars?" Martin said.

"No, it's a personal attendant," the man said.

Milo Gulchie rapped three times on the hardwood table with the back of his finger. The diamond ring on his middle finger made loud thumping noises. "Gentlemen, thanks to Lesmeck, our little setback has been taken care of, and we are now back in full operation."

"Yeah, since your link in the chain broke, Lesmeck, what have you done to make sure it doesn't happen again?" asked Lopez.

"I have added an extra layer of insurance. Instead of having only a lovely wife to worry about, both of the new couriers have a child to protect," Lesmeck said.

"You should have thought of it first. My sources in Botswana don't like not getting their money," Fidel Lopez said.

Lesmeck locked his fingers and looked at Fidel. "Well, you can assure your sources it won't happen again."

"For all our sakes, it had better not," Fidel responded.

Gulchie studied Lesmeck for a moment. "Tell us, where are the bodies?" he finally asked.

"Decaying away on the bottom of the Chattahoochee River," Lesmeck said with a grin.

Ruden slapped the table. "I don't like dumping bodies in the river. Things can go wrong and the next thing you know they're on the bank or lodged in a bunch of logs on the surface."

Milo grunted and said, "Any danger of their rising to the surface?"

Lesmeck grinned to each man. "Not unless they float wrapped with eighty pounds of chain. Ha ha ha ha."

They burst into laughter at Lesmeck's remark.

"Yeah, I hear the new couriers have pretty wives, too," Fidel said. "The kind my boys like to play with. Maybe you could introduce them sometime."

"To whom, those perverts? You and your men are pigs," Lesmeck said to Fidel.

Fidel turned to the big man. "You kill people, wrap their bodies in chains and drop them in the river and you call me and my men names?"

"Let me put it this way," Lesmeck said. "What I do, I do for business, but I have my limits."

Sunday, December 29th 1974

Chris yelled. "Mom, watch this."

Jennie turned in time to see her son catapulted off a mound of snow and sailed twenty feet through the air to a perfect landing. She clapped with amazement.

Chris came over next to his mother. "What did you think?"

"I thought it was magnificent once I got over almost having a heart attack. When did you learn to jump?"

"You remember yesterday, I told you I didn't feel like skiing. Well, I wasn't sick, but I didn't feel like skiing. I took lessons on how to jump, while you and dad were on the slopes. The instructor said I'm a fast learner."

"You be careful. We didn't bring you to Vail so you could break an arm or leg."

Robert appeared, skis in hand. "Well, I'm a fast learner. And I have learned skiing makes me hungry. Let's go in and have lunch."

Chris perked up. "I want some hot chocolate first."

Monday, January 6th 1975

On Monday morning, Robert Ludlow arrived at work an hour before anybody else and discovered half of the stolen sewing machines had been replaced. He looked along the wall the stolen fabric had left empty. One-quarter of his fabric had been replaced.

Robert inspected each piece of equipment. "Wait a minute," he said out loud, rushed to his office and returned to the sewing machines with some papers in his hand. He checked the serial numbers on each sewing machine against his original invoices and the lot numbers from the original packing slips for the material. His equipment had not been replaced. It had been returned; everything he was looking at was the same stuff taken during the break-in.

Robert was standing at his office door looking bewildered at the returned equipment and fabric.

From behind him came. "I think you should be back in business now, Robert."

Robert jerked around, startled at Lesmeck's sudden presence. "I didn't hear you come in."

"I saw your car and wanted to congratulate you."

Robert made a sweep of the room with his arm. "Did you have anything to do with my merchandise making its way back to me?"

"I had it delivered over the weekend. What do you think? Is it what you need?"

"Is it what I need? It's my stuff someone stole from me. How did you find it?"

"What a coincidence. I had no idea. My luck, I guess."

"Where is the rest of it?"

"It will be here in a couple of weeks."

"We need to call the police, so we can have whoever took it arrested when they bring the rest back.

And now I don't need your loan. How can I thank you?"

Lesmeck looked around the room. "You did get the loan. I purchased the machines and the cloth from a guy who had a big truck. How did I know it was yours?"

"What are you talking about?" Robert looked at Lesmeck's expressionless face. "You bring me my own stuff back and call it a loan."

"Look at it this way. I had to pay money for it. And you're back in business."

"I'm calling the police."

"I wouldn't if I were you."

"Well, you're not me."

"Call home first and talk to your wife. She may have company."

Robert rushed to the phone hanging on the wall and punched in his home number. "Hello, Jennie," he said when it was picked up.

"No, this is not Jennie. Would you like to speak to your wife?"

"Yes, I would, and who the hell is this?"

"I'm a guy fixing to have some fun."

"Put my wife on the phone."

"Robert, who are these men here? They—."

"Are you satisfied now?" the male voice said and hung up.

"Hello. Hello." Robert slammed the receiver in its cradle and turned to Lesmeck. "If they lay one hand on her, I'll—."

"Now, Robert, there is no need for anyone to get hurt. Hear me out." The fat man looked out into the room. "You owe me money for this stuff and all you have to do is fly up to New York and back once a week to show your appreciation. No need to pay the money back. Understood?"

"I'll see you in prison for this."

"My associate thinks your wife has a nice body. I could call and tell him to find out if she does."

Robert slammed Lesmeck against a wall with his hands around his throat. He let go with one hand and picked up a hammer. Then he felt like someone was inside him he didn't recognize. He had so much anger it frightened him; he had no control over himself like a stronger force was telling him what to do. "I'll bash your head in, you pig."

Lesmeck barely managed a few words. "You had better listen to me"

Robert eased his grip on the man's neck still holding the hammer up. "You had better start talking."

Lesmeck looked at his watch. "If I don't call my man at your home in three minutes, he will find out for himself how lovely a body your wife does have. Sometimes he jumps ahead of me. How long will it take me to get to the phone on the corner to make the call?"

"You bastard," He pulled the fat man off the wall and shoved him toward the door. "If he lays a hand on my wife, I'll kill him."

"Robert, I had no idea you were such a violent man," Lesmeck said, and walked through the door, down the steps, got into his car and drove off.

Robert ran to the door and watched Lesmeck stop at the corner, get out of his car and go to the pay phone. After a few seconds, he saw him get back in his car and drive off. Robert ran to the phone and called his wife. It rang only once.

"Robert," Jennie gasped in the phone. "Robert, I'm scared, please come home."

"I'm on my way, did he hurt you?"

"No, they are gone, please hurry home."

"Robert slammed the phone down and rushed to his car. The drive home seemed to take twice as long as usual.

Robert rushed through the door and wrapped his arms around his weeping wife. "What did he do to you? Did he hurt you?"

"No, I'm—scared, is all. I promise."

After Jennie settled down Robert told her about the equipment and material showing back up, and Lesmeck telling him he had bought it from someone.

"Let's go to Chris's school and check on him," she pleaded.

"Okay, but we don't want to frighten him. What can we do?"

"I'll take a lunch and say I thought he forgot it. I have got to be assured he's okay," she told Robert.

After finding Chris was at school and he was fine, they headed back to Robert's office. They got there as the plant foreman was walking in.

CHAPTER 4

Saturday, January 11ᵗʰ 1975

Roy's wife walked over and examined the machine. "Can you drive a forklift, Roy?" she asked.

"It's very simple," he said. "I've done it several times. My car should have been the last thing to go on. It's beyond me why someone would block it in like this." He stood by the freight moving equipment, staring at the pallets blocking his car.

Laura asked, "Is this going to be a common occurrence, you driving out of town, then having your car shipped back on a trailer so you can fly home?"

He climbed upon the forklift. "Yes, until I can afford a corporate plane, then I'll fly both ways." He reached down to start the engine.

Laura covered the key with her hand before he got to it. "I'm not sure I want you flying around in one of those small planes." She removed her hand.

"I could spend more time at home. Leave at nine for a noon appointment." He kissed her, then reached down and turned the key. The engine sputtered a few times before it started.

Laura elevated her voice over the noise of the engine. "Are you trying to get my approval?"

Roy leaned down and spoke close to her ear,

"Well, did I?"

. "Well, you do need one," Laura said, and backed away.

Roy revved the engine, until it smoothed out and pulled up on a lever lifting the forks off the floor. He drove to the back of the trailer and stopped to adjust the forks to fit the slots of one of the pallets of freight blocking his car, then he eased forward until the forks were in the slots. Pulling up on the lever raised the forks, and the pallet, then he backed up and placed it on the floor, then repeated the process with the other pallet. The trailer was the same height as the dock, so it was easy for Laura to drive his car off the trailer.

"Pull over to the ramp and ease down to the parking lot," Roy said.

Laura pulled to the ramp, stopped and got out. "Oh no, you can drive it off the dock."

Roy let the clutch out before the engine stopped. The machine lunged forward into a pallet of freight and caused a cement statue to break loose. It rocked back and forth a few times before it hit the floor and shattered. Roy got down from the seat and went to check the broken object.

Laura walked over, stood next to Roy and looked at the broken pieces. "How much will it cost you?"

Roy scanned the scattered remains. "Not much, it's a piece of concrete."

"It looked like a Flamingo to me. An ugly one to boot."

"Well, it was concrete before it was a big pink bird."

"Who buys those things?"

"Let's see." The cement made crunching sounds under Roy's feet as he walked over to the pallet the broken piece fell from.

Laura followed only to stop and go backed back when she got the same sounds under her feet.

Roy leaned over and looked at the shipping label. "It's from Lesmeck's friend down in Miami."

Laura cocked an eyebrow. "He's the guy you got the loan from. Are you going to deliver then to him?"

"It's always marked for customer pick up. A rental truck comes for it. There's a driver and Lesmeck. This came in last night. We don't open on weekends, so it'll be picked up on Monday. We should clean this up." Roy looked at the shipment. "Two pallets, twenty each, one out of forty, they probably won't miss it. As cheap as these things are, where's the profit in shipping these things?"

Laura leaned close to the floor. "Roy, there's some broken glass here." She picked up a piece of the glass and studied it. "This isn't— look, it's a diamond!" She stared at the floor. "There's another one, and another one. Wow, four, five, six... I count ten." She picked them up and searched around for more. "Where do you think these came from?"

Roy looked around. "I think I know where the profit is in shipping these things." He knocked over one of the concrete statues and watched it hit the floor and shatter like the other one. Among the broken pieces of cement, they saw shiny beads scattered around. "Yep, they came from these pink Flamingos. I'll be damned," he said.

Laura stared at the glittery dots. "How'd you meet this man?" Laura asked.

"I was sitting in my office one day and he came in and we talked. He said he could see we were a new company. Then he asked about the freight coming out of Miami. I told him we didn't have a lot. Turned out a friend of his had shipments coming from there. He asked if I wanted to haul it. After coming back a few times I let it out I had sunk a lot of money into the company, and I was struggling."

"Should you have told him?"

"He seemed like a smart businessman. I didn't see anything wrong with telling him. Anyway, he said he occasionally made loans. I thought about it and after a while, I figured, why not. It was him or the bank. So, we picked up his first shipment about ten days ago. They ship three times a week. This is the fourth shipment."

"I don't think your banker would have you transporting diamonds. I can't believe you made such a move without thinking it through."

"I'll have a talk with Lesmeck tomorrow. I'm going to put these diamonds in my office, and we'll get out of here. Follow me, my Dear. You know, diamonds are the best thing for a man's love life."

"There's on heck of a love life in your hand," she said as they walked to the office.

CHAPTER 5

Monday, January 13th 1975

When Roy got to work on Monday morning, he left word with his dock foreman he wanted to see Lesmeck in his office.

Thirty minutes after Roy took a seat at his desk The big man appeared at his open door.

"Your foreman said you wanted to see me."

"Come in. Close the door and have a seat."

The big man entered and took a seat in a chair in front of Roy's desk. "What can I do for you, Roy?"

"I accidentally broke a couple of your statues over the weekend."

"No need to worry about broken concrete."

"Breaking your freight didn't worry me." Roy tossed a paper bag on his desk. "It's what came out of them I'm concerned about."

The stunned big man picked up the bag and bounced it in the palm of his hand. "A rather pleasing sound wouldn't you say?" He poured twenty diamonds into his hand. Each stone was two to four carat. "Yes, they are very lovely. I must explain to my associates what happened." Lesmeck looked at Roy as though there was nothing unusual about the discovery of the contents in his hand. "Thank you for gathering them for me, Roy."

"Thank you, is all you have to say?" Roy said. "Do you know what would happen to you if I turned your stuff over to the police?"

"I think you know what would happen to you and your business if you did, right? I don't think you want anything to happen."

"Well, I don't. But I will tell you, I'll not be moving any more of your freight."

"It seems we had an agreement. You were to take my money and pay me back by transporting my goods from Florida." Lesmeck smiled.

Roy raised his voice. "You know I had no idea what you were into when I made the loan."

The big man fingered through the diamonds in his hand and picked out the largest one he could find and poured the others back into the bag. He rolled it between his thumb and forefinger and held it up for inspection. "Flawless and colorless, the quality of all my products, Roy." He extended his arm and dropped the shiny glass on Roy's desk. "I'm sure you can find a setting suitable for your wife."

Roy picked up the diamond and looked at it. "Put your bag over here."

Lesmeck put the bag on Roy's desk. "Sure, you want another one, earrings perhaps?"

"I don't think so," Roy dropped the rock into the bag.

The big man picked up his goods and headed for the door. When he reached it, he turned and calmly said, "Roy, you have no proof. I counted my statues. Two were missing. I have their contents in my hand and the rest are on my truck." He opened the door to exit but instead closed it back. "Let's not do anything foolish. You owe me a considerable amount of money. Read the small print. Could you pay me back today if I called in the loan? I don't think so."

Roy sat and stared at the big man, then the door after he left. Roy knew he was right; there was no evidence. His lawyers had gone over the loan papers before he took the money. The loan could be called in if he had reason to believe his company couldn't cover the payments. None of the company's customers were under contract, so they could have any company move their freight. Roy was sure he would be forced to pay off the entire loan as soon as he stopped moving his goods. He had used some of the money to purchase two new trucks.

Roy looked out his window and watched a black Jaguar drive slowly by.

Roy would have to tell Laura he would continue doing business with the man who had him hauling illegal diamonds. He began to think, "I need something to take the edge off. A little liquid courage will do the job. Or would it only add fuel to the fire, because Laure doesn't like me drinking and driving. Especially as much as I would need. The only time I overdo it is when I have a problem, so she'll know something is wrong.

He stopped off at a bar on Peachtree Street close to where Roswell Road forked to the left and went on up north. Roy went inside, walked over to the bar and removed his coat.

The bartender, a Scottish man named Ed Murry spotted Roy. "Your usual, Mr. C?"

"Sure."

No sooner than his coat was off an attractive, 5' 7" blonde. 5' 4" without her high heels showed up behind him, wearing a short red skirt and white top, cut low showing the top of her well-rounded breast.

"I'll hang it up for you Mr. Cobb."

"Thank you, Rita." He turned back to Ed. "Make it a double."

"You got it," Ed said. He put an ice-filled glass on the bar. While he added two shots of Chivas Regal, he said, "Hard day at work, huh?"

"Something like that."

"Well, here you are. A double for the trouble for a deserving man," Ed said.

After his second double, Roy threw four five-dollar bills on the bar. Rarely did he go past two single drinks. When he stood, out the corner of his eye Ed saw Roy sway and place a hand on the bar to sturdy himself.

Ed closed the register and walked over to his glassy-eyed customer. "Hey, Mr. C, those were hefty doubles, so I'm going to have my partner drive you home in your car. I'll have Rita follow in her car."

Roy looked around. "Not a bad idea. Thanks, Ed I'm embarrassed about drinking so much."

"Don't be. We've all been there, and it wasn't your fault, sometimes I get a little too generous when serving my good customers. You're not used to it. And that's a good thing." Ed Walked over to Rita and gave her some instructions.

Rita handed Roy his coat. "The cold air will help."

CHAPTER 6

Tuesday, January, 14th 1975

Cold wind blew cold across the dock sending a chill through Roy, looking through cobwebbed eyes, feeding coffee into his cotton mouth. He was wondering why last night he thought sticking his head into a spinning propeller would solve his problems. A product of the few more drinks he had after the ride home from the bar. Mild in comparison to his last hangover he remembered back in college, the next day after a tailgate party lasting well into the night. On a scale of one to ten, it measured at least a twelve. And on top of it all, he didn't tell Laura a thing.

Roy watched the freight from Miami being unloaded. "Be careful they break easy," he told the forklift driver when he backed out of the trailer with a pallet of concrete Flamingos.

The lift driver pointed across the dock. "The guys are here to pick it up."

Roy looked in time to see an eighteen-foot rental truck bumping the dock. He watched as Lesmeck got out, walked to the stairs and climbed them. The driver never got out. On two occasions, Roy had noticed the driver through the window. Each time he was wearing a different brightly colored coat.

"Good morning, Mr. Cobb," Lesmeck said as he approached Roy. "I see my freight made it without any breakage this time."

Roy looked at him incredulously. "You act as though our conversation didn't happen yesterday."

He ignored Roy's comment. "I should have another shipment coming in next week," then added. "I'll see you then."

"Damn you, Lesmeck."

"Not good a good way to talk to your customers?" The big man smiled, turned and walked off, not waiting for a response.

After considering the contract, Roy decided he would continue doing business as usual with the diamond hustler. Everything had gone fine so far. Roy figured, why rock the boat? Roy saw but paid little attention to the black Jaguar and its sandy-haired driver sitting across the parking lot.

"I'm going to have to continue doing business with the flamingo guy," Roy told Laura.

"Roy, I want you to know I'm strongly against doing business with him, and I insist you reconsider."

"I know, Honey, and it won't be for much longer. But for now, I'm in a tough situation. The loan is several months away from being satisfied. I'll have to move those damn pink birds until then."

Wednesday, January 22nd 1975

Laura slid across the seat to the passenger side when she saw Roy walking toward the car.

He opened the back door and tossed his

suitcase into the back seat, then he climbed behind the steering wheel. "Hey, Gorgeous, how's your day going? Give me a kiss."

Laura slid over next to him. "Great, now, you're home. I'm so glad I was able to cancel all my appointments today. How was your trip?"

"It was better coming home than leaving. You know how I hate being away from the two women in my life."

"Five days is too long for me, too," she said, and then inquired, "Is the new terminal up and running?

"Yep, like a well-oiled machine. The new terminal manager is going to work out fine." Roy put his hand out the window to signal a thank you to the driver of the dark-colored Jaguar who stopped to let him out. He thought, black Jag, what are the chances? How many people drive black Jaguars? He looked in his rearview mirror, but he was far ahead of it. I wish I had gotten a look at the driver.

Laura leaned into him and whispered in his ear, "Guess what I've got on my mind!"

"The same thing I have on mine," he said, and put a hand on one of her long, lovely legs that gave most of her 5' 9" height, then moved it past the bottom of her short skirt and rubbed her thigh. "You know those legs of yours were what attracted me to you?"

"I'll bet you don't remember the first time we met," Laura said, and nibbled his ear.

Roy's thoughts flashed back to the first time he saw Laura. "Hey guys, do either of you know the girl who played the last match before lunch?" He asked.

"What does she look like?" one of the guys asked. "We didn't notice."

"Oh, really, y'all didn't pay any attention to those legs and her mahogany, shoulder length hair? Well, I came face to face with her this morning. She was getting out of her car when she turned and bumped into me. She looked up at me with those pretty, green eyes that cover-girl face, and a gleaming smile. All you guys' eyes were glued to her on the court."

"Earth to Roy, hello, you sound like you're in a trance. We knew who you were talking about. The one with a centerfold body and long, pretty legs all the way up to her—."

"Yes," Roy cut in.

"It was obvious who you were talking about because you've been mesmerized by her all day. Her name is Laura Windsor. Why don't you go get her, guy? Since she never talks to anyone out of her league, and I'm not talking about tennis," the tallest of the guys said.

"Oh, one of those, huh? Well, we'll see. I'll bet you guys before the games end; I'll be talking to her. You wait and see." Roy told them, with a sure of himself grin.

Later after having a conversation with the hottest female to grace the courts, he went back to his buddies and boasted about making good on his word.

"Not only is she gracious and articulate, guys, she's intelligent. She's the total package," he told them.

"Well, I'll be darned, lover boy Roy. Aside for her family being well off, what else did you find out?" the comic of the group asked.

"She grew up in Buckhead. She attended a prestigious private school where she was an honor student, and a tennis star, at least good enough it earned her a scholarship to play the courts at the University of Georgia where she is now a sophomore." Roy twirled his racket in his hand. "Ha, ha ha."

"Okay, you might score. But tell me, what did she say when you told her you go to Georgia Tech?"

"Well, I may have blown it," Roy said, smiled and shook his head. "She told me, oh, I'm sorry, but I'll try not to hold it against you. Then it was time for her to go."

"Oh, no chance now, you should have waited before you mentioned G.T, man."

"You know, it was worth her being cocky, the way she shook her little butt as she left."

"Now you're talking," one of the guys said.

And that was how I met my wife. He came back to the present with Laure asking why he was so quiet.

"I was thinking. About us. Do we have time before Ashley gets home from school?"

Laura glanced at the clock in the dash. "Hmm, 2:30. If you drive fast enough, we can be home in thirty minutes. We'll have one hour and change."

"If you start undressing now," Roy said. "We'll have a head start." He stuck a finger in the top of her blouse between her 'D' cups.

"You keep dreaming," she said, and slid his hand away. "So, you had better match this car's speed to your motor."

"I'm off to the races."

Roy reached the bottom of the stairway as the front door opened.

"Come here, precious, give Daddy a hug," he said as Ashley hurried through the door after seeing her mother's car in the driveway. "How's my favorite twenty-two-year-old today?"

"Daddy, you know I'm only fifteen."

"Well, you're smart enough to be."

"Does it mean I am old enough to date now?"

"You'll never be, my dear. Well, maybe when you're really twenty-two."

Laura was halfway down the stairs. "I heard something about dating. Did your father promise you something I wouldn't allow?"

"Mom, what are you doing home?"

"I closed early today to be with you and your dad. That's the reason for starting my own business. Being able to close anytime and be with you two." She walked over and hugged them both.

Laura had put her accounting degree aside and started a secretarial staffing business two years after Ashley began school. It had grown to be one of the top staffing companies in the state, and she was in the process of branching out to several more states.

Roy never used his Chemical Engineering Degree; instead, he took the family trucking business and turned it into an interstate common carrier. They had rights to haul freight throughout the entire Southeast. Covering Mississippi, Alabama, the Carolinas, Virginia, Tennessee, Georgia and south into Florida.

CHAPTER 7

Thursday, January 23rd 1975

"Roy, will you come upstairs with me, please?" Laura's tone let him know it was a demand not a request. Roy behind her, she fast paced to their bedroom, taking steps that made her hair bouncing up and down. Once in the room she turned and faced him with a look cold enough to freeze a lit match. "How well do you know these people who have invaded into our home? I can't understand half of them. They're speaking every language except English."

"I know, honey, they're customers from work."

"Which customers are you talking about? The legitimate ones or the other ones? Don't tell me, I know the answer." Laura barely opening her mouth when she spoke. "I didn't like the way those two big Spanish men looked at me. I felt as though they were undressing me with their eyes, and they made some insulting remarks when I walked by them. Those women they brought are dressed like hookers. And the way they rub themselves on the men. I'm so glad we didn't invite our friends. You know who I'm talking about, the decent people in our lives? It's a blessing Ashley is spending the night out."

"It won't be much longer. I'll tell Lesmeck I'm

finished," Roy told her.

She gave her husband a stern look. "Please do, tomorrow," she demanded through gritted teeth. "God, I can't believe you brought them into our home." She shook her head. You're on your own. "I'm not going back down there. You should go now before they turn the party into an orgy."

Friday, January 24th 1975

Roy Cobb was on the south side of feeling normal when he opened the door to his home. In part from the champagne headache he was sporting. Adding to it, he knew he would have to cut his connections with someone he owed a lot of money. His expression changed to a smile when his daughter appeared in the foyer with a greeting. He was an expert at suppressing his problems when it came to his family.

"I like having those chimes go off throughout the house when the front door opens," Ashley said as she walked over and hugged her dad.

"How are the two most important people in my life?"

Ashley looked up at him. "Good," she said, "And how about the most important person in Mom's and my life?

"Couldn't be better, sunshine. How was your day?"

She smiled and waved her hands in the air. "I had a good day. Aced the English test I have been studying for."

Roy slipped his coat off. "I expected no less."

He walked over and opened the closet door. "Where's your mom?"

"She's in the kitchen. Is mom upset about something, Dad?"

He plucked a hanger off the rod and wrapped his coat around it. "What makes you ask?" He hung the hanger in the closet.

"She hasn't been herself today, so I was wondering."

"Adults get cranky sometimes."

"I won't. When I grow up, I'm going to be in a good mood all the time."

"Well, I hope you feel that same way as an adult. How're the driving lessons coming?"

"I get better every day. I drove home from the grocery store and not once did Mom have to correct my driving. I should be ready to pass my license test on my birthday."

"I'm sure you will, the very day you turn sixteen. Oh, I have to go back out. I got a meeting in one hour."

"It's I Have a meeting, Dad, not 'got' a meeting."

Laura made her way from the kitchen.

"Either way, I have to go back out. Wow, is my daughter going to correct my grammar for the rest of my life."

Laura kissed Roy on the cheek. "She may well. It's what you get for having such a smart child."

"I'm intelligent, Mom, and smart."

Laura and Roy gave their daughter annoyed looks but quickly turned them into proud smiles.

Taking it as a cue, Ashley changed the subject.

"You and Mom had a party last night, didn't you?"

Roy stole a glance at his wife. "It wasn't really a party. We had a few people over."

"Well, who left the wine bottle on the lawn?" his daughter asked before the doorbell rang. "Oh, I'll get it, mom, it's time to work on my school project. We'll talk about the party later." She left to collect her friend from the door and head upstairs, caring no more about the bottle she saw on the grass.

Roy cupped his fingers and tried to caress his wife's cheek.

She stepped back. "Who are you meeting?"

"Well, I said last night I would put a stop to you-know-what. You told me to do it tomorrow, which is today. Did you forget?"

She looked at him as if she wanted to run through him. "No, I haven't forgotten. And I do remember I asked you to stop a while back. Before those men came into my home and insulted me. Do you know how they made me feel? I'm your wife, Roy, and you brought those men around me. One of them put his hand on my backside. I don't know if I can forgive you. Thank God, it'll be over."

"I'll be glad, too. I don't know what I was thinking." He leaning down to give her a kiss.

"I don't think so." She turned away. "Will it be easy, telling him you want out?"

"Probably not, but I'm ready to find out."

"Well, I'm more than ready. I don't know if I care, but where are you meeting him?"

"Some place in Buckhead on Roswell Road called Buck's Tavern. Will you fix me a quick plate before I go? I shouldn't drink on an empty stomach."

"Sure, but only because I don't want it to go to waste." She adjourned to the kitchen, Roy a few steps behind her.

Roy sat at a breakfast table and ate his food.

He finished the last bite and stood. "The dinner was great. Kiss sunshine goodnight for me. I have a feeling this'll take a while. Lesmeck doesn't know when to give it up and go home."

"Well, don't be too late coming home yourself. I'll still worry. Oh, did one of our neighbors get a new car? I saw one go by twice today." Laura said.

"It's not my place to keep up with what other people drive. What kind was it?"

"Nice one, a black Jaguar."

"Are you sure?"

"Yes, I'm certain. The owner of the company next door to my office has a red one."

Roy had more things to worry about than cars as he left the house. She'll worry, he thought, at least she still has feelings for me."

CHAPTER 8

Friday, January 24th 1975

Roy parked a few doors down from Bucks Tavern, got out and watched a black Jaguar pull into a parking space across the street. When the driver noticed Roy looking at him, he turned his head away.

He stared at the driver for a moment before going inside. Roy found the big man and two other men at a table away from the crowd. "I thought you would be alone."

The plump faced man looked up. "Take a seat,"

Roy looked around, pulled a chair from under the table and eased into it. "Your kind o' place, huh."

"A couple of my associates." He pointed to a, thin, man dressed in a bright green suit over a gold shirt, a narrow-brimmed, green hat on his head. "This is Jay." He shifted his focus to the other man who wore a gray suit. "This is Martin."

"I'd like to talk in private, if we could, please," Roy's eyes were fixed on the green suit. He wondered if this was the man driving the rental truck

Lesmeck gestured to the bar with his head. Jay, over six feet, stood, pulled a foot-long gold chain from his coat pocket twirling it as he walked toward the bar with a distinctive bounce. Everyone in the place watched him until he put the chain away and took a seat. Martin acted as though he was used to the theatrics of the beanpole.

"All right, we're alone. What is it, Roy?"

Roy turned back around. "Is that normal?"

"For Jay it is. You want to talk?"

"You remember when we started our little partnership?"

Lesmeck picked up his drink. "Sure, I do; you were in the red with your freight business. I happened to come along at the right time and helped you out." He downed the remainder of the drink.

"And I appreciate what you did, don't think I don't." Roy leaned back and folded his arms on his chest. "But I don't need you anymore. I'm out."

"What do you mean, you're out?"

"I mean what I said. You remember when I found out what you were moving? Well, my wife was at the office helping me and she saw the merchandise. She asked me to—."

"What do you mean, she saw the stuff?" he interrupted. Lesmeck leaned in on the table. "You were too damn careless, Roy,"

"Careless or not, it's over. She wanted me to give it all up right then, and I told her I would. But I kept dragging—."

"You did the right thing," Lesmeck cut him off, "by not letting her ruin—."

"You don't understand," Roy blurted out, then rested his elbow on the table and put a hand up about six inches from Lesmeck's face. "At the party when she saw the kind of people I was dealing with—."

"What?" Lesmeck stopped him, looked around

and made sure no ears were listening. "What the hell did you expect? Preachers, big CEO's and the sort, people from your church choir?"

"Those two big goons from South America kept making indecent remarks to my wife."

"She's a pretty woman, Roy; men say things."

Not to my wife they don't," Roy blurted out. "Nor will they again. Do you understand?"

Lesmeck moved his hand side to side between them. "This is getting us nowhere. Settle down and let me explain something to you." He eased back in his chair and folded his hands in his lap.

Roy leaned back in his seat, locked his fingers in front of him and rested them in his lap.

"Most of us get what we want, one way or the other. Can you agree? Tell me how you get what you want, Roy?"

"By working smart, I like to think."

Lesmeck moved his head up and down. "Yes, I agree."

"At least it used to be. Now I think dissolving our relationship would be smart."

Lesmeck slowly moved his head side-to-side. He looked at Roy for a few seconds with a smile. His lips resembled a split sausage and turned inside out.

"Why are you shaking your head?" Roy asked.

Lesmeck smiled for a moment. "Let me tell you why. You know how I get what I want? I get it by helping other people get what they want." He pointed to the bar. "Take Jay, he likes to dress in easy-to-see clothes. It comes from feeling rejected all through school. The clothes get him the attention he missed. Now I pay him good money so he can buy those clothes. In return, he gives me what I want when I need it. Not really important you know what I need him for. You see what I'm talking about?"

Roy made short side-to-side movements with his head. "I'm not exactly sure I do see what some guy dressing like the Jolly Green Giant has to do with me wanting out?"

Lesmeck leaned in and put his forearms on the table. "Take yourself, Roy. We give each other what we want. Because I give in return, they give to me and the boys in Miami. It sounds like your wife wants you to stop giving."

"It's reason enough for me."

"Roy, if you don't give. I'll have to stop giving. If I do that, some people will get very upset, and I can say for a fact, you don't want them upset."

Roy quickly moved to the front of his chair, crossed his forearms on the table and stared Lesmeck in the face. "What the hell are you getting at?"

"Let me give you some advice." Lesmeck met Roy's gaze with a cold, stern look. "You go home and tell your pretty wife some people depend on your service. I have nothing more to say."

Tuesday, January 28th 1975

It was a project the students had been given. They had one month to put together a play. It had to be something new. The play they chose was about teenagers growing up in the 1970s. Ashley played the sister of a much older brother who grew up in the 1960s. Her part focused on how a sibling's perspective about the two decades was more understandable hearing it from each other than from the parents.

The older brother sounded out in a loud, stage voice. "Sis, in my teen years we had lots of influences to overcome. We had the hippies, drugs and changing music. We had the protracted war in Viet Nam to worry about. Young men and teenage boys were being drafted into the Army."

"Oh, how did you keep from going into the army?" The younger sister played by Ashley blurted out.

"By staying in school and going to college. Back then if you were not in school you were sure to be drafted to fight."

The play went on for two hours and received loud applause at the end.

As the crowd inched toward the exit, Roy was stunned when he noticed a plump man, sitting three rows from the doors, beside the aisle. He wore a smile, eyeballing Roy and Laura as they neared him.

Roy pointed across the room. "Look, there's Wilsons over there," he said to Laura, not wanting her to see the man. It worked, she turned her head, and they passed without her spotting Lesmeck.

"I didn't see them. Are you sure it was the Wilsons?"

"Maybe not, I think it was someone who looked like Jake." Roy looked back and saw Lesmeck was moving behind them. When they reached the lobby, Roy told Laura, "Why don't you find Ashley and meet me out front—no sense in both of us fighting this mob to get backstage."

Laura agreed and proceeded alone unaware of the plump man's presence.

Roy turned and faced Lesmeck. "Out front." He motioned to the door.

Both men pushed through the crowd and made their way out of the building and down the stairs. After reaching the sidewalk Roy walked to his left onto the grass about ten feet, stopped and turned around.

"What are we doing out here, Roy?" Lesmeck said.

Roy put a finger up in the chubby face. Through gritted teeth, he said, "What the hell are you doing here at my daughter's school?"

He had a grin on his face. "Roy, I have always been a fan of the theater.".

"I suggest you fill your niche somewhere else." Roy was jabbing Lesmeck in his chest.

"I rather enjoyed the play, Roy, especially the girl who played the younger sister. Wasn't she adorable? You know, now as I think about it, she had a striking resemblance to your wife. She wouldn't happen to be your daughter, would she? Very good figure—like Laura, wouldn't you say?"

"Damn you." Roy had him bent backward. "Don't push me too far."

Lesmeck had to take a step back to keep from falling. "Please, Roy, watch it. You don't want to cause a scene here. People might wonder what you have gotten yourself into. Thing about children, you have to protect them constantly. You know, from some lurking danger."

"Fair warning, Lesmeck," Roy was almost out of control. "I'll do whatever it takes to protect my family."

"Funny Roy. My friends feel the same way

about their business. Something to remember when it comes time to make the next pick-up. I hope you realize what I mean."

Roy gave him a shove almost putting him on the ground. "You pig." Roy turned and saw a black Jaguar drive past.

CHAPTER 9

Thursday, January 30th 1975

Inside a pizza restaurant on Peachtree Street in Buckhead, Roy was reading the daily newspaper. They occupied a table for four. Laura sat next to Roy and two empty chairs took up the other places. He noticed the couple two tables away from him and Laura. Every now and again the male would glance at them. Though only short quick glances, they did not go unnoticed.

"Roy, don't look now, but I think we are being stalked."

Roy folded the paper, placed it in a chair and casually looked around before he focused on the attractive couple in their mid-thirties staring at them. The man said something to the woman. She said something back to him. They both stood up. He was about six feet with sandy hair. The woman was blonde, another three inches and she would have been eye to eye with the man. They stepped away from the table.

Roy turned to Laura. "They're coming this way."

The couple stopped behind the empty chairs like they were expecting to be invited to take a seat.

Roy looked at the man first, then the woman. "Dear, we have company," he said to Laura.

Laura half-smile at the couple. No one said anything. The man's expression looked like someone who wanted to ask for directions, but didn't know where he wanted to go.

"May I help you," Roy said.

The man jerked his head as though he was surprised Roy would speak to him. "Oh, yes, I'm terribly sorry to bother you. I have something important I would like to discuss with you. Could we have a few moments with you and your wife, please?" He moved his gaze to Laura, then back to Roy.

Roy looked at Laura, who had her fingers locked together under her chin with her elbows on the table. Her mouth slightly puckered, and her brows went up.

"Sure," Roy said. "Please take a seat.'"

"Yes, of course. Thank you." The man scanned the room nervously before he pulled both empty chairs for underneath the table. After they were seated, the man wasted no time getting to the matter. "I don't know who y'all are, but I do know where you are headed. So, we can skip the introductions and get down to business."

"Let's not skip the part where you tell us who you two are," Roy said.

"My name is Robert Ludlow; this is my wife Jennie. First, I want to let you know I am taking a big risk talking about this."

"Are you sure we are who you think we are?"

"Yes, I'm sure. If you will give me a few moments."

"You got one minute to get my attention." Roy said.

"A minute is all I need, and if you don't want to hear me out, then we'll go. First off, I think y'all have made a big mistake."

"Me too, it was letting you two bother us. Your minute is up, please leave now or I'm calling the manager." Roy put his arm in the air.

"I drive a black Jaguar."

Roy eased his arm down. "You've been following me. You were on the street I live on. What do you want?"

"What I want is for you not to make the same mistake I did."

"I have no idea what you have gotten yourself into, and I have no desire to know."

"You need to hear me out, please."

"Your minute is about up," Roy said.

"Lesmeck's operation is what I have gotten myself into. I would guess the same way he has pulled you into it."

Roy looked at Laura, then back at Robert. "I think I have already made the same mistake you did. Keep talking."

"When I first saw you, I thought you and Lesmeck might be partners, and I wasn't going to say anything. Until the other night I saw you at the school and you had him bent backward. I figured then you might be in the same situation I'm in with him. Now are you convinced we need to talk?"

"You bought yourself some more time," Roy said.

"First off let me tell you. We are in the business of manufacturing pants. We make pants for several distributors. Lesmeck pulled a con on me is how I got sucked into this."

"Hadn't been in business very long, had you?' Roy asked.

"Yes, you're right."

"So, what do you do for our undesirable acquaintance?"

"I travel to New York once a week for him. I take the product up and bring money back. Not because I want to, but because I'm forced to."

"Why not go to the police?"

"I told the sleazebag I would. He said it was my word against his. He has some very dangerous friends, too."

"So, what does this have to do with me?" Roy asked.

"Maybe if you and I were to go to the authorities, we could prove we were forced into working for him."

"How did you end up working for him? Laura asked.

"Shortly after I started my business, my warehouse was broken into. All my material was taken. I didn't have insurance to cover it."

"And let me guess. Out of the blue Lesmeck showed up with an offer of a loan." Roy said.

"Not out of the blue. He had been by a few times. The first time he showed up, he said he was looking at a building in the area and noticed I was a new company."

"Sounds familiar, proceed."

"Well, after his second visit the break-in happened. He came by, and we got to talking and I told him about my situation. He offered to give me a loan. After I took it, he said I could do him a favor by making a trip to New York. Then it was another, then another. On my fourth trip I got curious and, on my way back I forced open the case. It was full of hundred-dollar bills. More than I had ever seen. When I confronted Lesmeck he offered me a pair of diamonds. 'Make a nice pair of earrings.' he said. Then he told me what I was transporting for him."

"He gave me a loan, too," Roy said.

The couple stood. Robert pulled a card from his shirt pocket and placed it on the table. "Call me after you have had some time to think it over."

After the couple left Laura picked up the card. "Do you want to keep this?"

Roy breathed out; his lips fluttered. "I guess it can't do any harm." He took the card and stuffed it into his wallet.

Monday, February 3rd 1975

At 6:30 p.m. Lesmeck walked through the door of Roy's office unannounced and unwelcomed. He took a seat in the chair across from Roy's desk, but he didn't bother to lean back. Getting comfortable wasn't what he was there for. He leaned forward and rested his forearms on Roy's desk. "Your driver failed to make the pickup on Friday. The boys in Miami are wondering why he didn't show."

"I instructed my terminal down there to stop picking up your freight, now you know."

"Do you remember when we talked about giving?"

"Yea, I do, a little. It had something to do with

everybody giving and receiving. Well, I'm through giving to your cause. So, you can tell your boys I've thought about it, and I want nothing more to do with your enterprise or your associates."

Lesmeck stood and leaned on Roy's desk. "Your decision for now is to not pick up my goods?"

"It's my final decision," Roy said without hesitation.

"I'll let my receivers know." He turned and walked out of the office.

Jay got out of the car and opened the back door. "How did it go, boss?" he asked.

His boss slid into the back seat.

Jay got in front.

"Get in touch with Miami, Jay. Tell them our Mr. Cobb will need some persuading."

CHAPTER 10

Thursday, February 6ᵗʰ, 1975

At 2:30 in the afternoon the intercom sounded in Roy's office. He pushed a button on the device. "Yes, Rachel?"

"Mr. Cobb, Mr. Hill is on the phone."

"Roy pressed the button for line one. "Good morning Charles."

"Roy," Charles Hill the Miami terminal manager blurted out. "I have some disturbing news," Charles told Roy about his morning.

"It did what? When? "How is Jacob?" After a few minutes of conversation, Roy told the caller, "Keep me informed." He sat for about thirty seconds holding the phone, looking at the wall, but not seeing it. He finally put the receiver in its place.

Thirty minutes before closing time Roy's secretary paged him, "Mr. Cobb, There's a news crew out here. They want to speak with you. What should I tell them?"

"News, what the—" Roy realized what it was about. "Send them in, Rachel." He straightened his tie and rolled his neck a couple of times before the door opened.

After the interview with Channel 5, Roy left the

office in his new Fleetwood and headed South on Moreland Avenue. When he turned onto Interstate 285, he tried to figure out where things had gone wrong in his life and what it would take to put them back the way they were. He wasn't sure how Laura would react to the news.

Roy pulled into his driveway, parked and went inside. For the past two weeks, he had not been greeted at the door by Laura. She was always doing something. This time, he found her in the living room with a magazine open about six inches from her face. Roy was sure she wasn't reading it she was using it as a tool to ignore him.

"I have something to tell you."

"It will have to wait until I finish reading."

"Is the article important?"

"I'm reading the entire magazine, and I'm on page one."

"It's business, related and it is very important."

After a brief moment, Laura closed the book and placed it on a table next to the chair she was comfortable in. She leaned back, placed a hand on each arm making it obvious she was not interested, but she would listen if he insisted. "Now, what is it you need to share with me?"

He told her about the interview with the news channel.

"Oh, Roy is Joseph okay?"

"He's in the ICU. Because the company's based in Atlanta, it will be on Channel 5 at six."

Laura glanced at her watch. "It's five minutes from now. I want to watch it." She stood, snapped around and walked to the other side of the room. "I'd rather Ashley watches it with us than hear it from someone else. Would you get her down here." She added, "Please?" After she realized her request had sounded demanding. "I'll get her myself, so I can prepare her on the way downstairs."

Roy watched Laura until she reached the top of the stairs and disappeared down the hall. When he saw them return to the stairs, he turned on the television and turned it to the right channel. When the picture came into view, Roy tried to take a seat on the sofa between his wife and daughter. Laura motioned for him to sit on the opposite side of Ashley.

"I want to be next to her," Laura said. She hid her ill feelings from Roy and their daughter's presence.

After a few minutes of local news, they heard, "And this from Miami. A truck belonging to Cobb Trucking, an Atlanta-based company exploded this afternoon in the parking lot of their Miami terminal. It happened when the driver tried to start the engine. He is in the hospital in serious condition. The reason for the explosion is unknown, although the police say it appears someone placed explosives in the truck. And now this…" Roy got up to turn the television off.

"Leave it on, Roy," Laura said. "I want to see the weather."

"Mom, Dad, is everything, all right?" The man said someone did it." Ashley's voice sounded stressful. "Why would someone want to kill one of Dad's drivers?"

Laura turned to see Ashley's worried expression matched her voice. "Oh, Sweetie, I don't know, but there's nothing for you to worry about, everything's going to be fine."

"It doesn't sound like your driver's fine. Does it, Dad?" Her words went soft.

Roy had walked over to gaze out a window at the street. He didn't hear his daughter. "I hired him. He was my first driver down there. I know his wife and son."

"Dad." Ashley said.

Laura reached for her daughter and put her arms around her. "Your father has a lot on his mind. Let me speak with him." Laura walked over to the window and stood beside Roy. "Ashley wants to asked you a question."

Roy turned around. "What, sunshine?"

"I was thinking—". Ashley looked at her mom.

Roy looked back at Laura.

"She's concerned about the driver's condition Is he going to be okay?" Laura asked.

"We don't know. Let's pray he will be. The Miami office will keep us up to date about his condition."

The phone rang. Roy picked it up, "Hello. Oh, hi, Charles," Roy said, and listened for a moment. "Good, thanks for calling." He ended the call and turned to his family. "Good news, my driver is going to be fine. He'll be in the hospital a few days. It'll be a week before he can return to work." He wanted to take their minds off the news. "How about dinner, I'm a little hungry."

"It's ready," Laura said. "I have to set the table. It'll be done in five."

"I'll help you, Mom."

"You can fill the glasses with ice and tea, it's on

the counter." She told Roy, "It looks like she wants something else to think about."

After a meal with no mention of the Florida incident, the three of them settled into a quiet evening at home. When bedtime rolled around for Ashley, Laura followed her upstairs.

Returning twenty minutes later she took a seat on the opposite end of the sofa from Roy. "Ashley wanted to talk about the truck when she got into bed. She's also worried about all of us. It's good she was tired; she fell asleep easily." Her voice became firm, "Roy, is there anything else I need to know?"

"Yes, there is. Lesmeck came to my office on the first of the week. He was upset about my truck missing a pickup."

Laura sat silent for a moment. "Do you think he had something to do with the explosion?

"I don't know."

"I thought you were finished with him."

"It's not the way he saw it. If I wait it out by not making any pickups. They'll have to get someone else."

"It doesn't seem like he wants someone else. He wants you," said Laura.

"Hon, don't you think it's been long enough?"

"Long enough for what?"

"Can't you let go of what happened at the party?"

"What, those perverts putting their hands on me."

"I mean don't you think—?"

"Yes, I think. About how you have turned our lives upside down. And how horrible it is what has happened to our company and it showing up on the news." She wasn't looking at him.

He opened his hands and moved them up and down as he spoke. "How long are you going to treat me this way?"

"As long as it takes, is how long."

He stood and walked toward her. "What do you mean?" He turned and went back to his seat, and told her, "I know, I know, Honey, I'm sorry."

"I'm trying, Roy, believe me, I am. But I can't turn these feelings off and on at will."

Roy, being an athlete, and his several years of martial arts training had always been a rock, difficult to shake. He was capable of handling any physical or verbal threat with an uncommon calmness. It did not include the treatment he was receiving from his wife. The blow she was delivering was one he could not deflect. It was like a punch to a glass jaw.

CHAPTER 11

Friday, February 7th 1975

"Mr. Ludlow, the last three money drops have been short. Can you explain why?"

Nervously Robert answered, "I don't know anything about being short. I swear."

Lesmeck pulled opened the oven door on the gas stove. "I find it difficult to believe. Maybe I'll take care of you now. Then I'll ask your wife when she comes home."

"No, she doesn't know anything about it either. You have to believe me. She doesn't know. Neither of us does."

"Ah, come on, you expect us to believe you," said a slim dark-haired guy wearing a pinstriped suit. He bent down and looked in the oven. "What you been cooking in there, Bob. I'll tell you what we're going to cook in there. Shish-ke-bob head. Get it, ke-bob head." He burst into laughter. "Ha ha haaa haaa. Ke-bob head." He slapped Robert on the back of his head.

"Oh, meet Angelo Gulchie, Robert, he's Milo Gulchie's son. You know Milo, don't you? He's the gentleman who gives you the money you turn over to me."

Just as Martin pushed Bob's head into the oven the door sprang open, hiding Jay between the open door and the wall. The men snapped their heads around.

Jennie was pointing at thirty-eight. She moved it from one to the other, then she looked at her husband on his knees. "What's going on?"

"Mrs. Ludlow, I'm glad you're here. We were discussing money," Lesmeck said.

"Money? What do you mean?" Jennie said.

Lesmeck shook his head "It seems your husband has grown greedy in the last few weeks."

"Yeah, greedy is what you can't be with my dad. Makes him look bad to the other guys, and he don't like looking bad," Angelo said.

"You've been getting all your money. I don't know what you're talking about," Jennie said.

"Jen, get out of here. Now please," Robert Ludlow pleaded.

"Not without you. Get up." She pointed the gun at Angelo. "You help him."

"My arm hurts, I can't lift anything," he said in a smug tone.

Jennie fired her weapon at Angelo grazing his arm. "Now I know it hurts," she said.

Angelo cried out. "Awww, you bitch you'll pay for this."

"Robert can you get up?" she asked.

"Yes, I can," he answered and slowly started to get to his feet.

She pointed the gun at Martin. "Help him, or it won't be your arm I hit," Jennie said.

"Okay, don't lose control." Martin reached

down and took Robert's arm.

"A little more and we're out of here baby doll," she said.

Robert got to his feet and leaned on the counter. "Let's go, "He said and walked toward his wife. His steps were slow and small.

"A couple more steps and we'll get out of here," Jennie said.

"Yea, yea a couple of steps my ass. You are a dead woman, you hear me bitch," Angelo said.

Roy reached for Jennie's hand, and she reached for his.

All Jennie saw was a yellow flash before the door slammed into her. Jay reached out with his long arm, grabbed her wrist and pushed it upward. Angelo lunged at Jennie, grabbed the gun and twisted it out of her hand. She felt two long arms wrap around her and move to her breasts and squeeze them.

"Wow not bad. I think I'll take her into the bedroom," Jay said.

"Leave her alone—."

Angelo smacked the back of Robert's head with the barrel of the pistol he had taken from Jennie. "If I want anything outta you, I'll knock it out of you, ke-bob. Like I just did, only harder. Now shut up."

Angelo placed the gun on the counter, then using his uninjured arm he slapped Jennie across the face with the back of his opened hand. "I told you bitch."

Jay, in his bright yellow suit, was massaging Jennie's breasts. "Hey, I'm playing here, stop with the slapping. How about it boss, can I take her to the bedroom?"

"Jay, what am I going to do with you?"

"I don't want you to do nothing with me, boss. I want her to do it to me, so what'd you say?"

"Go ahead, Jay, go ahead. But keep the noise down."

Angelo brought the pistol down across Robert's head knocking him to the floor.

Jay pulled a struggling Jennie through the door.

"Can I go too, boss," Martin said.

Lesmeck moved his head side to side. "How did I end up with you two perverts?"

"What's a pervert?" Martin said.

"Please go. Angelo will entertain—ke-bob, until you two get back."

"Oh, boy," Martin said, and followed Jay. "Boy, it sure is fun being a pervert, ain't it?"

Robert raised an arm. "Wait a minute guy, you got this all wrong, I never took any of the money, I swear to you, Lesmeck."

Angelo came down across Bob's jaw with the butt of the gun. "Shut up and listen to your wife enjoy herself."

Bob heard his wife's frantic screams.

Angelo put his face next to Robert's. "See, I told you she would like it."

Robert began to weep before another blow to his head sent him into total darkness.

Angelo doused a glass of cold water into Bob's face. "Wake up, Bobby. Your wife wants to tell you what a good time she had."

"Bobby, Bobby." Jennie crawled naked across the floor reaching for her husband. "They hurt me so bad, baby. I fought them with all my strength. I promise I did."

"I know you did." Bob took his wife's hand and pulled her to him. "Let me hold you."

"I don't think so, asshole." A shot rang from the pistol in Angelo's hand. The bullet pierced Jennie's head and lodged in her husband's chest. "Hey Bobby, your wife checked out without saying bye."

"Bastard, you, bas——."

Another shot rang out and the inside of the oven turned red with splatter after the bullet passed through Robert's head.

"Hey, I thought we were going to cook him," Jay said.

Lesmeck shook his head. "Gentlemen, let's take a seat."

"Take a seat? What for? We should get out of here," Angelo said.

"Trust me and take a seat," Lesmeck said. "We're waiting for someone."

The men finished their work and sat in a car ready to pull out of the driveway.

"You would think if you pay a man enough to afford a house like this, he will respect you and not steal from you," Lesmeck said.

"How much did he clip you for?' Angelo asked.

"Out of the last few shipments, he took to your father he only returned enough money to cover eight diamonds instead of the ten."

"Wow, no," Angelo said. "You didn't know?"

Lesmeck turned and look at Angelo. "Know what?"

"My old man only got eight diamonds in each of the last few runs. The guys in Miami cut him back so they could send some to a new customer."

They all looked at each other.

Lesmeck stared at Angelo who was in the backseat next to Martin. "You mean you knew all along he wasn't stealing from me, and you said nothing?" Lesmeck's voice went up several octaves. "We killed those two for no reason."

"I didn't know why we were here. I went along for the ride," Angelo said.

Slowly Lesmeck moved his head from Angelo to Martin to Jay, until he was staring out the front window. "Ha ha, ha ha. "Gentlemen weren't it fun, though." he began to laugh heavily.

Jay laughed. "Yeah, the wife was nice."

Martin, then Angelo joined in with laughter.

"I didn't like having to wait around after we did it," Martin said.

"We had to do what we felt was necessary," Lesmeck said. "Let's go, Jay, I think we all need a drink."

CHAPTER 12

After closing, Roy was sitting in his office, relieved his wife was finally coming around and talking to him. She even gave him a peck on the cheek before he left for work.

He had about the same feeling he did the first time he dated her. Roy leaned back in his chair, rested his feet on his desk and placed his hands behind his head and lost himself in thought, it was Wednesday before Thanksgiving, the last year of college when fate took over. Their paths crossed in Buckhead.

Roy walked out of a store right into Laura's and a friend's path. "What a surprise, seeing you off the courts; what are you two girls up to?"

"I could say the same thing," Laura responded, and added comically, "We're trying to get up enough nerve to fight the uptown traffic so we can shop at Rich's."

Roy jumped at the opportunity to spend some time with her. "Well, this happens to be your lucky day, ladies. I'd like to go shopping uptown myself. So, I'm volunteering my driving services to the two of you."

After a couple of hours of shopping and conversation, he asked Laura for a date.

"A date with you," she sounded surprised

He picked her up at seven o'clock the same evening. They managed to squeeze in three dates before they had to be back in school. It was their last date Roy hadn't tried to kiss her.

As they walked out of the movie on Sunday night, Laura told Roy, "I can't believe it's time to go back to school already,"

"Times flies when you're having fun," Roy said as he opened the car door for her. They drove back to Laura's house, making small talk about their plans after graduation.

After Roy told Laura's parents goodbye, Laura walked him back to the front porch, flipping the porch light off on their way out. Outside she faced him in the dim light and stood still.

"Umm, Roy, how many times have you taken me out now?

"Uh, three, counting this time," he said.

"Well, don't you think it's time you—."

"Yes, it is," Roy answered before she finished, took her by the shoulders and pressed his mouth to hers. She closed her eyes and parted her lips. He wrapped his arms around her, she relaxed in his strong arms. He held her for what seemed like a long time before they parted.

"What took you so long?"

"I don't right off kiss every girl I date."

She gave him a little jab in the ribs. "Every girl?" she said.

"I almost did it the first time I took you out."

"Nope, second time, I would have let you," she said.

His good mood ended when Lesmeck brought

him back to the present time by walking in without knocking and stopped in front of his desk.

"Don't bother taking a seat, you won't be here long enough to get comfortable," Roy said as he pulled open the top drawer of his desk and gripped a pistol with his right hand.

"What I have to say I can say standing, Mr. Cobb."

"What, we're not no first names anymore?"

"I want to talk in a business nature, so first names are out. You can take your hand off of your pistol, too. I'm not armed." He opened his coat, turned around, then closed it. "I didn't come here to harm you."

"I suggest you say it quickly and be on your way." Roy eased his hand out of the drawer but left it resting on the rim of his desk.

Lesmeck looked at Roy's hand resting over the drawer. "Oh," he said, pulled the liners of his pockets out and stuffed them back in. "I see you had some trouble on the southern end of your business. Makes you think, doesn't it?"

"Think what, Lesmeck?" Roy snapped, not moving his right hand.

"If I were you, Mr. Cobb," Lesmeck was rocking from heel to toe, hands in his coat pockets. "You should think. Was what happened to your poor driver because of something you didn't do? You also might be thinking; making the pickups from now on would be a good idea."

Roy pressed a button connected to the bottom of his desktop.

The latch on his office door engaged with a

thud. Lesmeck looked, then back at Roy. "Very clever, but for what reason?"

Roy closed the drawer. "Keeps the riff-raff out." He leaned back, spread his fingers and put them into a steeple. "Most of it anyway. I'll tell you what did pop into my mind. What happened might have been some of your handiwork. I've ordered around-the-clock security for my terminal. So, I won't be making any more of your pick-ups."

"Yes, I got word of the guards. It seems you are on top of things. You know, Miami is a very large city to have trucks running around in."

Roy leaned forward, placed his elbows on his desk, made a fist with one hand and wrapped the other around it and rested his chin on them. "What we haul is interstate freight. Stuff crossing state lines gets the FBI involved without me saying a word. Tell me this, how would it feel having the Feds breathing down your neck?".

Lesmeck removed his hands from his pockets, leaned down and rested them on Roy's desk. "I think you are on to something, Mr. Cobb. None of us want their involvement, including you. Besides, I could think of more important things a man should worry about."

The garlic breath Lesmeck sported from lunch encouraged Roy to lean back. "What the hell are you trying to say?"

"Tell me, how are your lovely wife and pretty daughter doing?"

Lesmeck straightened up when Roy jumped to his feet. The back of Roy's legs hit his chair sending it backward into the wall. Roy walked around to the man and stopped inches from him. Towering over him, Roy put a finger in Lesmeck's face.

"You leave my family out of this you, son-of-a-bitch. They had nothing to do with what you and I had going on. Did you notice that I said, had? You come near my family and I'll—." Roy didn't know exactly what he would do, but he was sure he would do something. "Stay the hell away from them."

"Some things are out of my control, Mr. Cobb, remember."

"I think it's time for you to leave. For good."

"Are you sure?" Lesmeck asked.

"Yes, my last words to you and your friends." Roy pointed at the door.

Lesmeck stared at him for a few seconds. "You know, you said your wife felt uncomfortable around those two men at your party. They are recipients. I hear they are dying to see her again. You might want to think about it."

In an instant, Roy delivered a four-finger jab to the throat of the plump man. He grabbed his throat and gasp. Roy put his fingers around the man's neck and tighten as his opponent tugged trying to pull free. The vice-like grip wouldn't budge. He pulled at Roy's hands as they went tighter, his lips parted, and he made choking sounds. His eyes were opened wide and rolled upward; he turned white. When the struggling stopped, Roy realized what he was doing and let go. Lesmeck fell to the floor, gasping for air. Roy took a seat on the corner of his desk. He rubbed his hands together, curled and straightened his fingers a few times.

"Damn you caused me to almost kill you. I 'm

not so sure I'm glad I didn't."

"Do you think—this is the—last of—this?" Lesmeck barely pulled himself to his feet and leaned on a chair. "I'll—give you—until Wednesday—to change—your mind."

"Get the hell out of here. You two-bit thug. I'll finish the job if you come near my family." Roy thrust a finger at the plump man.

Jay, standing beside the car wearing a purple suit, opened the back door and Lesmeck got in. The engine never shut off, so the interior was warm. Jay closed Lesmeck's door, then got in behind the wheel.

"You, uh, tell him off, Boss?" Jay glanced in the rearview mirror. "Man, you don't look so good—you okay?"

"Damn—him."

"You got something caught in your throat?" Jay asked.

Lesmeck put a hand up and motioned for him to drive away. Jay made a right turn out of the parking lot and got a horn blast from a car after it did a lane swap to keep from hitting them.

Jay gave the driver the finger and shouted, "Bastard, where'd you get your damn license, Sears Roebuck?" He floored the gas and swore to be damned. "I'll show the son-of-a-bitch."

Lesmeck slapped him on the shoulder a few times. "Jay, Let—it alone."

"Sure, Boss, the jackass is not worth it anyway."

After several minutes, Lesmeck got his voice back. "Mr. Cobb is a more stubborn man than I expected. I think it will be easier to convince his wife."

"Oh, yeah, she's a looker. I think it would be a

good job for me and Martin, boss?"

"Those two big South Americans should be very persuasive. And I understand Mrs. Cobb is already acquainted with them. Call Miami tonight, get them up here."

"Ah, are you sure you want them? I'd like to have a crack at her. You know, if those guys mess up," Jay turned his head to face his boss.

"Watch the road, Jay. We'll have to see."

Roy came out of the room he used as a home office thinking about today's event. He walked into the sitting room and found Laura on the sofa reading a book.

When she saw him, she closed the book and placed it next to her. "Let's watch the news."

"Is it that time already?" he said and pulled out the knob on the television. "Maybe something has happened." He walked over and took a seat beside Laura as a commercial ended.

The news anchor started talking. "We have an update on a story from yesterday. The Atlanta police said they have notified the next of kin of the double murder victims discovered over the weekend. The names of the couple are Robert Ludlow and his wife Jennie Ludlow. Their thirteen-year-old son is in the hospital in critical condition."

Laure's face was frozen on the screen. "How horrible for a child to lose his parents. And in such a terrible way."

The newscast continued. "According to the evidence at the scene, Atlanta, police think the man and woman were killed Friday afternoon and whoever did it waited for their son to get home from school and shot him. Right now, it is unknown if the victims were a targeted or a burglary gone terribly wrong."

Roy got up and turned it off. He turned and faced Laura, who possessed a freighted look.

"What's wrong?"

She didn't answer for a moment. Then she said anxiously, "Roy, aren't they the couple we met at the pizza restaurant."

"Oh, no," Roy reached into his back pocket. "I think you're right." He brought out his wallet and fumbled in it. "Where is the card he gave me. Here it is." He pulled the card from his wallet. "Yes, it is."

"Oh, my God, I can't believe it. They're dead." Laura began to shake. "Where's Ashley?"

"She's upstairs in her room."

Laura jumped up, hurriedly climbed the stairs and rushed into her daughter's room and to the child's bed. "Ashley." She raised her voice, "Baby."

Her daughter lay still.

"Baby," Laura said frantically, and grabbed the girl's shoulders and shook her.

"Mom, what are you doing?"

Laura put her arms around her daughter. "Nothing, hon. I wanted to kiss you good night. I lost my footing and fell on the bed."

"You're holding me too tight."

"I know, baby, but I want to." She descended the stairs looking back twice at Ashley's room.

Roy met her at the bottom step. "There is no way nobody could have gotten here without the alarm going off."

"How did they get into the Ludlow's house?"

CHAPTER 13

Tuesday, February 11th 1975

"Thank you for getting to this today," Roy said.

"It's good you called first thing this morning before I got started on another job. Dispatch marked your request "Urgent" and we always put those first. Those motion sensors will pick up anything from a human to a medium size dog. When it does, your system will place a call directly to the police," the technician said as he handed Roy a copy of the work order. "Sign here, please."

Laura and Ashley walked in the door as the alarm company truck pulled out of the driveway.

"Ashley, take your new clothes to your room and hang them in the closet," Laura told her daughter.

"What did she get?" Roy asked.

"She had to have a new dress for the Valentine's Day Dance at school. I think she has her eye on a boy in her class." Then she asked, "What's going on? The man leaving in the truck said he installed some sensor equipment in the house. Why do we need all the extra security?"

Roy walked over to the wet bar and picked up a bottle. "Lesmeck came by the office yesterday. He made some threats." He picked up a glass, poured a double shot of scotch, gulped half of it down, and told Laura about his conversation with Lesmeck. He left out the physical altercation.

Laura looked at him in disbelief. "All the talk about you waiting him out was all bull crap, wasn't it? Those two men he mentioned, what did he mean? Are they going to harm me or Ashley? What are we going to do?"

"I've got to think of something." Roy downed the rest of the drink. "I have my forty-five in my briefcase. I'll be taking it everywhere I go. I've hired two bodyguards for you and Ashley. They've been watching y'all all day."

"I'll have to drive Ashley to school and back. We can't confine ourselves to this house every day after Ashley gets home. She'll ask questions and I don't want to frighten her. You had better come up with something, yesterday."

His voice came harshly at her. "I know it, damn it. Let me think." He refilled his glass.

She walked over to him. "You have never snapped at me, Roy, and I don't want you to start now. I don't think you'll find the answer in a bottle, either."

He poured the Scotch into the small sink and took her in his arms. "I know. I'm sorry."

She pulled away and gave him the same look she had at the party. "I'm scared, Roy."

Wednesday, February 12th 1975

Laura and Ashley left home with two cars following them. One stayed at Ashley's school until her mother picked her up. The other went wherever

Laura went. Roy went to work packing his pistol in his briefcase.

Nothing unusual happened during the day and the Cobb's were back at home after Ashley's class let out. She was disappointed she couldn't visit with friends or have one over for the afternoon. All her mother told her was they wanted to have the afternoon for family time. Although the reason disappointed her she accepted the idea.

Friday, February 14th ,1975

Ashley reached the bottom of the stairs. "How do I look?" she asked and did a complete circle in her new dress.

"You look lovely. As a matter of fact, you look like your mother," Roy said, and thought, almost a carbon copy of Laura, except for the lighter hair color, courtesy of his genes, she was a head turner for the boys,

The family left the house the same as the day before, going in the same directions with the same cars following them.

Work was out of the question for Laura. After dropping Ashley off at school, she decided her home would provide more comfort.

At home Laura was exhausted when she sat down on the sofa. After a moment, she eased her head down on one of the fluffy pillows and a moment later she was asleep.

"What's your business here, fellow?" The man sitting in the car looked up to see a man in an Atlanta

Police uniform.

He pulled his wallet from his pocket. "Privat Investigator. I've been hired to keep an eye on a house." He pointed to the Cobb home.

Laura opened her slumberous eyes suddenly and sheepishly pushed herself up to a sitting position. Her eyelids eased back together, she suddenly opened them and thought, did I hear something. A sound filled the air. Looking around she realized it came from the front door. She glanced at the clock. It was 10:30, two hours from the time she had got back home. The chime sounded again, then again.

"All right, all right, I'm coming," she said, and rubbed her eyes. She slowly got to her feet and walked to the door. Through the ornate glass, she saw a blue shirt. She peered through the small round cylinder spotting the metallic shield. Not thinking twice, she opened the door. "What can I do for you, officer?"

There were two men were grinning. With a Spanish accent, one of the men said, "Anything you want to."

She gasped. "What are you doing at my house?"

Lesmeck stepped from beside the door. "Mrs. Cobb, I see you remember my friends. They have come all the way from South America to pay you a visit."

Laure tried to slam the door shut but Lesmeck caught it and used his body to push her back into the room, two men following him. He looked at the men and pointed to the upstairs.

"No, no, please leave me alone," Laura begged.

The man in the uniform spun her around and

wrapped his arms around her, finding her breasts and squeezing them. "You are so fine, lady. I wanted to do this at your party. I think we will have a good time."

Laura remembered the man's heavy accent. "Stop, oh dear God, please stop."

He picked Laura up and headed up the stairs. "What do you mean stop? We haven't started yet."

Lesmeck walked ahead of the two men looking in each room until they reached the end of the hall. "This is her room. Bring her in here."

The man threw Laura on the bed and ripped her blouse off. The other man tore her slacks off and threw them on the floor.

"Oh, wow. Yes, you are fine," the man who pulled her slacks off said, and pulled some rope from each pocket. "You will enjoy this." He cut the rope into four pieces and tied one end of each piece to her hands and feet. Then he tied the other ends to the bed's four posts. After he had her secured. "So soft," he said as he ripped her bra off and massaged her breast, then ran his hand over the rest of her body.

"I want to enjoy her too," the other man said, and began to rub her body.

Lesmeck stepped to the side of the bed. "Enough for now," he told the men. "Mrs. Cobb, I could let my friends continue. However, I am willing to intervene if you tell me you can convince your husband to fulfill his part of our arrangement."

"I will, I promise I will. If you leave me alone."

"Let me leave you with something to think about, in case you change your mind. These two gentlemen here. Oh, how silly of me for calling them something they are not. A gentleman would never treat a lady this way. Anyway, they have a fondness for young girls, especially girls say, around fifteen years of age."

Laura's head shook frantically. "No, no, I told you I would. I'll tell him and he'll do it."

"You do look rather vulnerable lying there. A pretty inviting position, but they'll wait and see." They left Laura spread eagle on the bed, as if she were doing a jumping jack exercise and froze in midair.

The front door flew open and in rushed a lady and the private investigator from the car out front. Both had their guns drawn.

"Mrs. Cobb," the lady called out. "Mrs. Cobb." She called again. "You cover this floor, I'll check upstairs." They moved through the house. The lady looked in all the upstairs rooms before she reached a closed door at the end of the hall. In one quick motion, she turned the knob, opened the door, darted in, crouched with a gun pointed and panned the room and searched the closet. She was shocked to see Laura tied spread-eagle, on the bed wearing only black panties and a gag in her mouth. The lady walked to the bed.

She leaned over and undid the knots and removed the cloth from Laura's mouth. "Mrs. Cobb, my name is Robin, I'm with the investigation company hired to protect you." Robin heard movement in the hall and walked to meet the investigator's footsteps at the door.

Her hand shot up. "Stop. She's okay, she needs a few minutes."

"I'll wait downstairs." He lowered his gun.

"We'll come down as soon as she's ready." Robin gathered Laura's clothes up from the floor. The buttons were missing from the blouse; the zipper was ripped from her slacks.

Laura's head was buried in the pillow as she sobbed. After a few minutes, she sat up. The investigator handed her a towel she had retrieved from the bathroom.

"Those damn pigs," Laura said. "I don't have time to dwell on this. I have to get up." She looked at the expensive garments now reduced to rags. "I'll get something from the closet." She eased off the bed. Tears tried to form in her eyes, and she almost cried again, but stopped. "Hell, no. They can threaten me, but I will not let them break me."

"Mrs. Cobb, we need to call the police."

"No, I've got to go to my daughter's school, now." She hurried to the bathroom and showered. After her shower, she went into the closet and dressed.

Before they left the room, Robin looked at her. "Mrs. Cobb, I hate to ask. But did they?"

"No, they didn't," Laura said, shaking her head. "They said they would save it for the next time."

"We'll make sure there's not a next time," Robin said. "Let's go get your daughter."

Once they were downstairs Laura told them what the men looked like. "Let's go to my daughter's school. I'll have to take my car. Ashley won't know what to think if I show up in a strange vehicle."

"I'll ride with Mrs. Cobb," Robin told her partner. "Follow us—radio our man at the school— tell him we're on our way, Code Red."

The ladies lead the way with Laura breaking

every traffic law she could without putting them in danger; an accident would delay them.

"Mrs. Cobb, did they threaten your daughter? If they did, I understand why you're in a hurry?"

"I told you they said they were saving something for the next time. They were not talking about me." Laura took a corner on two wheels almost. "Open the glove box," she told Robin.

Robin opened the compartment. "What the hell. Can you use this?" She reached in and pulled out a military Browning 45 1911 automatic.

"As good as any man and I will."

"How did you learn to shoot?"

"My father, Bird Colonel Robert Windsor, US Army retired."

A red light at a major intersection stopped them. Robin's partner pulled alongside them, rolled down his window. Robin did the same.

"The girl's okay, our man spotted her and some other kids eating lunch outside on the school grounds. He's thirty feet away, on alert." The light changed and Laura sped away, leaving the man as he tried to tell them they could slow down.

"She'll be fine. Code Red means don't let her out of your sight. Our man has the descriptions of the two men who attacked you, so he knows what to look for."

Laura reached Ashley's school before lunch was over. Because the dance was the last hour, and a half of school Laura didn't want to check her daughter out early.

CHAPTER 14

The women talked until school was over, then Robin left Laura and got in the car with her partner.

Ashley opened the door and sat down. "The dance was great, Mom. Guess who asked me to dance first." She used a bubbly tone.

"I don't have to guess. I can tell by your smile who asked."

"Yes, and we danced most of them together. He danced some with other girls but that was okey. I danced with other boys," she told Laura as they drove off with Robin and her partners behind them.

Laura turned to speak to her daughter.

Ashley cut her off. "Mom, how did you get that bruise on your face?"

Not knowing it was there, Laura glanced in the mirror. There was a blue, almost black, wide line going from her chin up to the right side of her face. "Would you believe I ran into an open cabinet door?"

"You should be more careful, Mom."

At the Cobb house, the two men and Robin were introduced as business associates of Laura's. Ashley entertained her mom and the three strangers with stories about the dance.

"Robin, let me show you the upstairs," Laura said. "Ashley, would you get the gentlemen some coffee?"

"I would love to see it," she said. As strange as it seemed, Robin knew Laura had a reason for inviting her to see upstairs. The women left Ashley with the two men and headed off.

Once in her bedroom, Laura said, "Help me get the buttons off the floor. It would be difficult to explain if Ashley were to find them. I'm also going to dispose of these clothes."

"Here you go, take these. I have all five of the buttons," Robin told Laura, then said, "I don't know how you can be as strong as you are."

"It's not easy. How did they get past the man outside my house?"

"One of them was dressed in a cop uniform. You can get one at any costume rental."

"Really, they look so real," Laura said, sounding surprised. "I opened the door because I thought the man was a policeman. Damn. They should have a label on the shirt saying, 'I'm a 'phony'."

"It would have been helpful," Robin said. "

"Did your partner see them come to the door and wonder why they were in my house so long?" Laura asked.

"Our man said during the conversation he was struck on his head. Someone must have opened the back door and clobbered him. I found him tied up and gagged. He had been out about thirty minutes when I found him."

"Really, it seemed more like hours," said Laura.

"I'm sure it did. Luckily, we always check on each other as a safety precaution."

"You've not mentioned your husband the

whole day. Don't you want to call him?"

"My husband, you're right. All I could think of was Ashley." Then Laura confessed. "The truth is. I feel my husband's the cause of this. He put our lives in danger. I can't say anything further."

Shall we join the others," Robin suggested.

After a brief time, Robin left for home and the private eyes took to their cars so they could keep an eye on the house.

Ashley heard a car pull into the driveway and ran to look out the window. "Mom, Dad's here." She went to the door to meet her father.

"Well, hello, sunshine. How was your day?" Roy knew she wanted to tell him something. Rarely does she greet him at the door. He was right. She told him all about the dance.

Laura emerged from the den. "Hi, how was your day?"

"Wow, what happened to your face? Let me look at it." The mark was darker than when Ashley brought it to her attention.

"She ran into an open door. I told her to be more observant," Ashley said.

Later, with dinner out of the way and Ashley fast asleep, Laura sat next to Roy on the sofa trying to decide which approach would be best to present her husband with the event from today. Finally, she figured the best option was to come out and tell him. So, she did.

"Honey, why didn't you call me so I could have been here for you?" Close to tears himself, he cuddled her in his arms. "The mark on your face, it's from the man attacking you, isn't it?" Roy couldn't hold his wife close enough. He felt helpless. "I hired those men to protect you, and they can't tell a phony cop from a real one. How damn stupid could they be."

"I was fooled too. I opened the door for him."

"You're not a trained private investigator, either. He is. I'll get somebody else."

"No, I like the lady, and I trust her. I think they'll be more alert from now on. Besides, how can you be sure anyone else wouldn't go to the police?"

"You're probably right. If you trust them, they are okay with me. I hate the thought of those men handling you, ripping your clothes off. I'll kill them for putting their hands on you, seeing you naked, tying you up."

Laura backed away from him. "They didn't see me totally naked, honey. I told you. I promise."

Roy clutched his fist. "Are you sure you are not telling me so, I'll—."

"Please," Laura interrupted. "Don't make me defend myself for what those horrible men did to me, please."

The phone rang. A life saver, she thought. It saved her from the agony of reliving the nightmare.

"Who could it be?" Roy said.

Laura headed to the kitchen to answer it. "My mother is the only person who would call and she is on an airplane right now."

"If it is, her says hello for me," Roy said, and headed upstairs to check on Ashley.

Laura was debating. Her inner self was saying don't answer the phone. Her outer self got the best of her. "Hello," she said.

"I enjoyed our little get-together today. Did you, Laura?" The voice said. "You have a beautiful body."

"Who is this? You bastard, sick son-of-a-bitch."

"Now, Laura, I paid you a compliment. I'll bet your daughter has a very nice body. She looks a lot like you."

"Bastard, bastard," Laura said frantically into the phone. She slammed the receiver down and backed away with her hands on her face, almost in hysterics.

Roy walked into the room. "Honey, what's wrong? Who was on the phone?" Roy tried to pull her hands down."

"No, no, don't touch me." She backed away and steadied herself on the counter. "You're the cause of all this, anyway. It's all your damn fault."

"Laura, please tell me. Who was on the phone?" Roy pleaded. "It was them, wasn't it?"

"They threatened our daughter. They're sick people, Roy, sick. I'm going to check on Ashley. Please go out and check on the men outside."

"I came straight from her room, she's fine."

Laura rushed past him. "I'm checking again."

Roy went outside and talked to each man long enough to assure himself they were wide awake.

She told Roy when he came back inside, "I'm scared. If they do something to Ashley, I don't know what I'll do,". Then she asked, "Are those men alert?"

"They're fine, Honey. Let's sleep in Ashley's room. What little sleep I'll get. By the way, your comments earlier were true. It is my fault, but we have to get through this together."

The doorbell sounded, causing Laura to jump

next to Roy. "Don't answer it," she said.

"They're going to have a man in the house tonight. This must be him."

"You don't know for sure. Look first."

Roy went to the door and peered through the round hole. "It's a woman." He opened the door.

"Mr. Cobb, my name is Robin."

Before she could finish introducing herself Laura appeared next to Roy. "Come in Robin." Laura looked at Roy. "She's from the agency you hired. I told you about her."

Robin stepped inside followed by a man who must have been six nine. "This is Jim; he'll be your house guest for the next few nights."

He was muscular. He may have been bigger than both of those South Americans, definitely bigger than one and a half of them.

Jim put out a meaty hand. "It's a pleasure to meet you Mr. and Mrs. Cobb."

At first, Roy and Laura didn't say a word. They stared up at the giant.

Roy finally shook the man's hand. "Oh sorry, Jim, yes it's good to have you in our home. Right, Laura?"

"Oh, yes." She looked around for a chair she could give up if the man's weight outmatched it. "Please have a seat. Over there." Laura did a hand gesture to a chair she had never liked. Her aunt had presented it to them when she and her husband sold their house and retired to Florida.

After a few minutes of talking, Robin stood. "I'm outta here. The guys out front will stop anyone from entering your house. If they do make it inside, they'll have to deal with Jim."

Laura thought, I hope they make it inside. Maybe Jim could tie them up. We have a ball bat in the garage. But she said, "Thank you very much, Robin."

After getting acquainted with Jim, they felt safe, so they went up to Ashley's room. Roy walked to her bed and stared down at the sleeping teen.

Everyone fussed over the Cobb and Windsor families' first grandchild. She'll have Cobb for her last name. She has to have Windsor in her name, Laura's father told his daughter and son-in-law.

Her first name can be Windsor, Laura's mother had said.

Laura told her mother; it would be confusing.

Windsor will be her middle name Roy had told them

Laura was pleased with the solution and told them, "Mom, Dad, Roy has it all figured out. She'll have both names. Leave it to my husband—he always has the answer." When she was five days old Roy's father wanted to know when we were going to give her a first name.

"Soon, and when we do, she'll be 'Whoever' Windsor Cobb." Is what they were told.

CHAPTER 15

Friday, February 15th 1975

Roy was right; neither he nor Laura got a good night's sleep. They wanted to be out of their daughter's room before she woke.

Keeping everything from Ashley had proven to be much more difficult than they had imagined.

Roy and Laura made the trip to Ashley's school. Upon returning home, they were greeted by Robin who was standing beside her car in the driveway. After they were introduced to two fresh supersized bodyguards, Robin told them she would be spending the day with them. Laura was comfortable talking to Robin, so her presence was welcomed.

They all went inside and planned the day. It was decided two men were needed at their home and two at Ashley's school. No one mentioned the events of the previous day. Probably neither of them wanted to be the first to bring up the unpleasant issue.

By the time lunch rolled around, Roy decided his wife was safe, so he headed to his office. His company was applying to the Interstate Commerce Commission for an expansion of rights to cover both Illinois and New Jersey; and he would be meeting with lawyers to finish the paperwork.

"I would like to ride with you, Mr. Cobb, if you're okay with my tagging along," said Robin.

Roy looked at Laura.

Somewhat surprised and a little disappointed, Laura said, "Fine with me, I guess. I'm sure I'll be okay."

Once in Roy's car and on their way Robin said, "Mr. Cobb, I won't ask you what it is you have gotten yourself into. But how are you handling all this?"

"Please, call me Roy, and thank you for not asking any questions. I think I'm doing pretty well for a man who has had his wife manhandled and I don't know what else done to her."

"Your voice sounds like you don't believe your wife's account of what happened. "I'm sorry if I upset you. And I'll use your first name. If it's any consolation, I asked Laura, and she said they did nothing to her," Robin added, "I believe her. She isn't acting like a woman who has been raped. I think they only wanted to send a message."

Roy shifted his grip on the steering wheel, twisted his hands on it and spoke. "I believe her. Why would she lie to me? It's the thought of—you don't understand." Roy tightened his lips.

"It might be important that you let your wife know you believe her." Robin's words left him empty of conversation. "Thank you," is all he said.

On the drive to her office, Laura thought how awkward it was to have someone follow her everywhere.

She worked through lunch right up until time to leave and pick up the younger Cobb.

At day's end, everyone was sitting around the

dinner table. Robin and the two hefty men enjoyed the home-cooked meal.

After dinner, the two men were replaced by a fresh duo who would spend the evening at the front and rear of the house. Jim walking through the door was a welcomed site.

Roy retired to his study to go over the day's unfinished work. Laura and Robin took seats in the den. Their conversation included Laura's business and how Robin entered her profession.

"My father was a career FBI agent. He put a lot of the mob away," Robin told her.

"You have a tough father like I do. He taught you how to shoot?" Laura asked

"Yes, and how to spot the bad guys?".

Laura rubbed her hands together. "Okay, bad girl, listen. I know what I am going to do. Let me tell you." The women sat on the edge of the sofa one foot on the floor and one leg bent resting on the sofa.

"Don't tell me you have some elaborate scheme planned?"

Laura took a deep breath and let it out. "I told you my father was retired from the Army. He was in the Infantry. He was in Korea when his retirement came up halfway through the Korean War. Then, he spent ten years in the Army Reserves. During his Reserve time, he attended their sniper school. While there he became friends with a soldier with whom he has stayed in contact with. When they talk, it's Army this, Army that, everything. My father loves to relive those times and apparently so does his friend, who was in Vietnam. My father learned through him a few years ago about some men who did special raids in Nam.

They now work as a team rescuing people who have fallen into the hands of rebel groups in other countries."

Robin got a gleam in her eyes. "Tell me about them. Are they here in Atlanta?"

"Oh, yes, but my father doesn't know how to get in touch with them. Today when I spoke with him, I asked him about them. I didn't tell him why, and he didn't think anything about it. He likes talking about his old friends."

"Have you told Roy about them?"

"Yes, but he thinks they're something my father's friend has fabricated. Like a fairytale."

"Well, real or not, what good are they if we can't find them?" Robin said.

"Well, fortunately." Laura shifted her body and began to tell Robin. "He told me one of the team members took a job last year at a club in Buckhead."

"Why would he want to work in a club?" Robin said.

"Probably to have something to do, I guess. Let me think about what he said. The friend told him he was going to visit the club around October after he retires from the Army. He gave me the name if the club." Laura thought hard. "What was the name of the place? Shit. Excuse me, it slipped out. What was the name he told me? He said it was a country and western place."

"Damn, can't be but one of those in Buckhead," Robin said.

"Don't you know it? Ah ha, it's "The Missing Link." I'm going to pay the club a visit tonight. I know the name of the guy."

91

"Oh, well, it sounds good. You be careful," Robin said, thinking the same as Roy about the team of men. They're a myth. She got up and told Laura, "I'm 'outta' here. I have an early appointment. I'll tell Jim you're going out. One of the men will follow you. Look, I won't be around very much for a while. I'll be monitoring what's happening with you guys, so good luck."

"Thank you for being here, Robin." Laura got a handshake, and she was gone.

Roy poked his head through the door. "I'm off to bed." He looked around. "I didn't know Robin had left," He walked into the room and remarked, "Robin doesn't mind asking questions, does she?"

"No, she doesn't. What did she ask you?"

"Nothing, really, how I was doing, and uh, nothing else. I do want you to know I believe what you told me about those men."

"I'm glad you do. It's important to me that you do."

"I'll see you upstairs," Roy said.

"I'll be a while, don't stay awake for me. I have some papers to go over."

Midnight, after her shower, Laura dressed and checked on her husband. His slow breathing assured her he was fast asleep. She eased down the hall to check on Ashley. Once downstairs, she told Jim, "I'm going out for a while."

He gestured an okay and said, "One of the guys will follow you."

"It's what I was told." Laura went into the kitchen, pulled her car keys off a hook and went into the garage. With a light touch on a button the garage door quietly raised. She backed the Cadillac out and stopped beside a keypad on a post long enough for her to tap in a four-number sequence and down the door went down. Then she was off to Buckhead; one car in tow.

Laura found the club parking lot full. She spotted a driveway on the side of the building and took it to the rear parking lot. She parked in an empty space, turned on the interior light and pulled the mirror down to reflect her face. She did a lipstick check; hair adjustment and she was ready. Then she thought, "Damn, this is a country and western club. Why am I worried about my looks? The women in there have probably been dancing all night." She got out and headed around the building to the front.

Her shadow had parked three spaces from her car, got out and was following twenty feet behind. "Mrs. Cobb, are you going in there?"

Laura stopped at the front corner of the building and waited for the man. "Wait here and watch the front door until I come out. I shouldn't be long," she told him, and proceeded to the entrance. The closer Laura got to the door the stranger she felt. A blanket of fear began to wrap around her. She began to think about what those men did to her in her own home. They could have listened to the conversation I had with my father. They knew I was coming here. She felt their hands on her body.

"Don't panic, Laura," she told herself, reached the door and stopped, her body trembling. She asked herself, "Am I crazy? I'm going to enter an establishment I have never heard of, looking for a man I have never heard of and don't know if he even exists." She conjured up a tiny bit of nerve and slowly opened the door, stepped into the small foyer and stopped. She moved to a place on the wall and leaned back against it. All I have to do is open the door. I can hear the music.

The door opened and out walked a couple with an arm around each other's waist. The man looked at Laura and in a slightly intoxicated voice said, "Well, it looks like you had one too many, are you holding that wall up, or is it holding you up?" The couple laughed as he opened the door, and they were gone.

I had better go in before I lose my nerve. She stepped to the door and opened it, stepped far enough inside, so the door could close behind her. I'm trapped, oh shit. What am I doing in this music, smoke-filled, dimly lit large square cube?

She stood still, inside shaking. It's a good thing the lights are low. No one can see me. Something inside her said, "Get the hell out of here." She disobeyed the voice and moved a few steps into the room. A hand touched her on the arm, causing her to jump and rotate her head. She saw a white-haired gentleman's grinning face. Do I look as frightened as I am, was going through her mind?

The face spoke. "Two dollars cover, please."

Laura stood mouth open, eyes wide. What did he say? Did he say come with me? I won't go with him. I'll scream.

The man held up two fingers. "We charge two dollars to come in, ma'am."

She sighed with relief and put a hand on her chest. "Oh," she said. He spoke English, not Spanish. What is the matter with me? "Yes, of course, you charge to get in. How much did you say?"

He held up the same two fingers and said, "Two bucks."

"Two dollars is all?"

The man nodded. "Unless you want to pay more."

"How much more?" Laura said.

"Just give me two dollars."

He's a joker. No, he's flirting with me. Laura dug in her purse, came out with a twenty-dollar bill and presented it to the man. "Do you have change?" I wonder if he's an old country singer.

"I'll see if we've taken in enough tonight." Still smiling, he pulled Andrew Jackson from her fingers and passed it on to a lady sitting at the cash register. The lady took the bill from the man and held it up to the light. She opened the cash register but didn't put the twenty in. She laid it on a narrow shelf above the drawer and dug out three fives and three ones and handed them to the smiling man, which he fanned out and held them up. Laura took the bills and thanked him. After she confirmed her change was correct, the lady placed the twenty-dollar bill in the drawer.

"Where can I get a drink?" Laura asked the man.

"We sell them here at the bar."

"I'm asking for it, tonight, aren't I?"

"A little." He looked across the room. "Oh, hold on, the bar is crowded. Here's a waitress. What would you like?" He motioned for a girl walking close to them carrying a tray.

"Scotch and soda please."

"A call brand or bar brand?" he asked.

A call or bar brand, what the hell is he talking about? "Give me something good."

He told the waitress, "Chivas and soda."

Chivas. Is it a call or a bar brand? It must be a call brand because he had to call the name out. I've had Chivas before.

The waitress headed to the bar with the order.

This guy can't be who I'm looking for, he has too many years on him. She turned her focus to the dance floor and all the couples slowly dancing. She thought, those people look like they're doing foreplay out there. The drink should settle me enough to collect my thoughts.

In less time than it would have taken Laura to get to the bar, the girl made it over and was back with her drink.

Harold lifted the drink off the tray. "One Chivas with soda." He presented it to Laura.

"Thank you, how much?"

"Don't worry about it, my treat for causing you to jump when I asked you for the cover charge."

"Thank you, you're very kind. Give this to the waitress." She held up one of the five-dollar bills. He pointed to the tray. Laura put the bill on the flat disc.

She got a big thank you. A signal that the tip was larger than she was used to getting.

Laura looked back at the man. "I didn't realize my nervousness was so noticeable." She took a good-sized swig from the glass. "Wow, what a strong drink," she said.

The man laughed. "You're not much of a drinker are you."

"No, but, whew, I guess I needed it," she said.

96

After a smaller sip she asked him, "Do you mind if I stand here for a few moments?"

"Pretty as you are you can stand by me all night. Step over here out of the traffic," he told her, with the same grin he used for her reaction to the drink.

Laura blushed. "Thank you." She moved close to the counter. "Can I rest my drink here?"

He put a napkin on the counter. "Sure, put it on this."

After a few more sips, she felt comfortable. Between his friendly smile and the drink, she was working up enough nerve to ask about the guy she came to see. Does the guy even exist? Well, I'll never know. So, here I go. She didn't look at the man when she asked, "Does a Cody Billings work here?"

"Cody Billings?" he said, and then he went silent.

I knew it. He doesn't work here. There probably no such person. Damn me, damn me for coming here.

"Sure, he works here," she heard.

Laura looked at him with a surprised stare. "He does?"

"I'm sorry, but the cashier got my attention when you asked me. You did ask about Cody, didn't you?"

"Yes, I did."

He looked across the room. "There he is over there." He pointed to a towering, well-postured statue on the other side of the room.

"May I go over and have a word with him?"

"You can, but he isn't near nice as I am."

"It would be difficult. You are a hard act to

follow. I hope to see you on my way out." Laura gripped her glass and weaved through the crowd and crossed the floor. When she reached the other side of the room she stopped and took a couple of deep breaths. She thought, what will I say to him? Hi, stranger, I need your help to take out some bad guys. Might have worked eighty years ago. I'll play it by ear. She approached Cody from his right side. "Mr. Billings."

He paid her no attention.

"Mr. Billings." She noticed his eyes were fixed on the crowded room. Laura followed his stare and saw she was competing for his attention. The formidable competitor was a pair of white, tight jeans, standing by the bar. When Laura put her hand on his arm, she felt a muscle so hard she doubted if he felt her touch. She rose up on her tip-toes close to his ear, giving her field advantage over her opponent. "Mr. Billings," she blurted out. "May I speak with you, please?" Laura was used to looking up to her husband when she talked to him, but Cody, not as tall as Jim, had at least two inches' height on Roy.

Cody Billings turned to face her. "Speak with me? It sounds as if you have something specific you want to talk about."

"I do, Mr. Billings, if I could have a few minutes of your time."

"Right now, I'm sort of busy."

"It looks as if you are only standing around doing nothing. Is that busy for you?" She remembered what the man at the door said, He isn't nice as I am.

Cody looked around, then back at Laura. "Can't argue with you there. What do you want Miss—."

"Cobb, Laura Cobb. My father knows someone who knows about the other work you and your friends do."

"You mean, Harold, the guy at the front door. The work we do here."

"No. Your other job, Mr. Billings."

"What do you mean? This is the only work I do."

"I know this is not the only thing you do, so don't play dumb with me, I am no idiot." Laura was not sure what kind of reaction her remark would bring.

"No, I don't believe you're an idiot, maybe I don't understand."

"Look, my father is a very responsible person. He is retired from the Army."

"What is your father's name?"

"Colonel Robert Windsor. He was a Bird Colonel. He claims to have a reliable source who he met at sniper school."

"I don't know anyone from sniper school."

"I know you and your friends were in Vietnam, and y'all did special work over there. I also know you and your team help people who are in trouble."

"Okay, let's assume you're right. What do you need?" He put a hand up. "Hold on. Let's go outside." Cody led her across the room to the front door. He stopped and said something to Harold, then he pushed the door open for Laura.

"Thank you, Harold," Laura said when they exited.

Harold smiled big. "Come back anytime."

CHAPTER 16

When they passed the big bodyguard, Laura told him, "We're going to my car, I'll be driving back home shortly." They continued to walk.

"Is he yours?" Cody asked.

"He's watching over me. The reason he is, is why I want to talk to you.

The big fellow followed them down the parking lot until Cody and Laura reached her Cadillac. When they got in he went to his car and stood beside it.

Once in the car, Laura wasted no time telling Cody about her and her husband's situation.

"Mrs. Cobb," Cody began, "you are asking me and my friends to do something we can't do. Work for dirty money."

"You don't understand what we're going through. We have a daughter who is so sweet, and we love her very much. They will hurt her. Please understand!" Laura begged.

"If you know about us, and I believe you do, you have a reliable source, which means you know we sometimes work for the government. If they were to find out we worked for money coming from what your husband does, it would be all over for us."

Laura turned on the inside light, dug into her purse and pulled out a photo. "Look at this, she's my little girl." Laura was in tears. "Look at it." She held it up to his face.

Cody focused on the photo. "I see, Mrs. Cobb, she's very lovely." He paused, then said, "You said a truck exploded in Miami. The two men who broke into your home are from South America. The diamonds would have come from Africa into South America, then Miami to here, then probably all up the East Coast."

"I don't know where anything comes from or goes. I want it to stop."

"How did your husband get mixed up with them?"

"The company was in the red. Roy had over-spent while building it up and somehow this man, Lesmeck, showed up out of nowhere and offered to help Roy out with a loan. He seemed nice enough, my husband said."

"It's the way they work. They sucker you in and never let you out. I'll tell you what I'll do, Mrs. Cobb, I'll check on these men from South America. They shouldn't be too difficult to get a line on. I'll have to do this free of charge."

"Thank you very much, and call me Laura, Mr. Billings."

"I will if you'll call me Cody."

"Well, Cody, how will you get word to me?"

"How did you find me this time?"

"Of course," Laura said. "I had better go. I hope my husband doesn't wake up."

Saturday, March 1st 1975

As the days passed, they saw no more of Lesmeck's boys. Then after a week of being followed around, against his wife's better judgment, Roy halted the private security the first day of March.

"Roy, I don't feel safe letting those men go."

"I'll keep them if it makes you feel better."

Laura sighed and paused. "No, I have to move on. You did the right thing."

The night after Roy let the security guards go Laura went back to the club, then again two nights later to follow up with Cody Billings. The first time he said he didn't have anything to report. On the second visit, he was off for the night. Laura let go of the notion he would find out anything. She doubted he even tried.

Saturday, March 15th, 1975

A couple of weeks passed and the guy at the club crossed her mind. What was his name, Laura thought. Cody, yes. I wonder if he found out anything. Huh, he was probably glad to get rid of the crazy woman who came to him with some outlandish story. I don't think I'll ever be able to open my door for anyone, ever again.

Everything seemed fine for the Cobb family and Ashley had grown tired of staying home. Laura dropped her daughter and some friends off at the movies. It was Roy's job to pick the girls up from the theater.

Roy sounded worried on the phone. "Honey, I

can't find Ashley," he told Laura. "Her friends came out about fifteen minutes ago. They said she went to the bathroom, and they haven't seen her since."

"What are you saying?" Laura said, panicked.

"I knew letting her go to the movies was a bad idea."

"Roy, I'm getting dressed. I'll be right there." Laura broke the connection. Before she got out of the room, the phone rang.

She hurried to pick it up. "Hello, Roy, did you find her?" she blurted out without waiting to see if it was Roy.

"Laura, you sound anxious. Did you lose someone?"

"Who is this?"

"Never mind who I am. What is important to you is who I have. Listen."

"Mom, Mom, help me, come get me, please." The words horrified Laura.

"Ashley, baby, honey, where are you? Laura said. "Honey, I'm coming to get you, where are you?"

The man's words were chilling. "Don't waste your time, Laura. Your daughter is going on a plane trip. I'm sure she'll enjoy South America."

"No, no, please don't' take her. Let her go. I'll do anything. How much money do you want? Take me." Laura pleaded. "I know who you are, I recognize your voice," she said, trying to come up with something they'd swap for her daughter.

"I'm afraid it's not going to be, so easy, Laura. Your husband had his chance. It's too late now. The man spoke slowly.

"No, it can't be too late. He'll pick up your

stuff, I promise. When do you want it picked up tomorrow? Yes, he'll have it picked up tomorrow. Please," Laura pleaded crying into the phone.

"The people in South America are angry with my friends in Miami. My friends in Miami are angry with me," His voice grew louder. "And *I am* angry with your husband. So, everyone is angry, and Roy is last in line. I'll be in touch, Laura." He hung up. Laura, hysterical, ran and got dressed.

"Roy," she said, grabbing his arm. "They have Ashley. Lesmeck called. He said they're taking Ashley to South America. We have to do something; I want my daughter back."

"Come with me, hurry," Roy said. They ran to Laura's car; he turned to her. "What are you talking about?"

Laura had him by the arms, shaking him. "I want her here, now."

"How do you know this?" He put his hands on her shoulders and squeezed them.

"Roy, you're hurting me, stop," she said, sobbing. "Lesmeck let me talk to Ashley. She was frightened. They're taking her away. I tried to reason with him." Laura's body went limp. She fell and hit her head on the asphalt.

"Oh, Laura, are you okay," Roy said, but got no response. He scooped her up in his arms, opened the door to her Caddy and put her in the front passenger seat.

CHAPTER 17

Sunday, March 16th 1975

Laura sat up. "What time is it?" she asked. "Where am I?" She looked around the room. I have to get out of here. "What time is it?" She tried to get out of bed.

The nurse was holding her down. "You're at Piedmont Hospital, Mrs. Cobb."

"The hosp—, how did I get—, what happened?"

"Your husband said you fell and hit your head. You got a nasty bump up there," said the nurse.

"Mrs. Cobb, do you remember me," came from a male voice.

"Who are you? Wait, I know you. You're from the protection agency. Where is my husband?" She looked at the nurse. "Did he leave me here?"

"He said he had some business to take care of. I'm supposed to stay with you and not let you out of my sight," the man said.

Laura looked at the nurse. "I'll be fine; you can let go of me now. I was confused when I first woke up." Laura eased back down on the bed. The nurse slowly eased her grip on her.

"I'll be back in a few minutes to check on you. I

have to make my rounds now."

"My daughter," Laura said, and touched the bandage on her head only to quickly withdraw her hand. What time is it?" she asked the man.

He checked his watch. "One twenty."

"I have to get out of here. Is my car in the parking lot?"

"Your husband took it, I think. I'm supposed to keep you from leaving."

"No, what you said was you are to stay with me. Do you have a car? If not, call us a taxi, now."

"I have a car. Where do you want to go?"

"Do you remember the club we went to?"

"Yeah, it was on Roswell Road."

"Well, we're going there."

"Mrs. Cobb, if you want a drink, I'll get you one, but I don't think you should leave here."

"I'm not going for a drink. I need to talk to a man who works there. He can help me." Laura stood only to sit back down. "Woo, help me up, please."

He lent a hand to steady her. "Maybe you shouldn't get up."

She stood. "I'm okay. I tried to move too fast. Go get your car and meet me out front."

"I can't leave you, Ma'am."

"Well, will you please leave the room so I can get dressed? We don't have much time, so you need to get your car while I get ready. I'll meet you out front."

"All right, you sound determined." He walked out.

Laura looked in the closet. The only thing she saw was her long, black leather coat. She removed her hospital gown and put the coat on over her panties and bra. I'll need two dollars. She checked her purse for money. Good, more than enough. She glanced at the table beside the bed. What's this? She picked up a folded piece of paper. This is Roy's handwriting, 'Your blouse had blood on it and your skirt got dirty when you fell. I took them, will bring more.'

Laura buttoned the coat and went out into the hallway and got on an elevator. When she got off on the ground floor, the man was waiting for her at the door.

"How long will it take to get there?" she asked him. "They close at two, I can't miss him."

"Going to be close, but I think we can make it," he told Laura.

"We'll have to make it."

They pulled into the club parking lot at two o'clock.

"There he is getting in his car," Laura said. "What kind of car is it?".

"Mustang, 1970 Mach 1 to be precise."

"Can you follow him to his home?"

"I can, but this time of morning he'll know we're tailing him."

"Well, let's do it anyway, he might not pay any attention to us." They took off behind Cody Billings. "Don't lose him," Laura snapped. "Sorry, I didn't mean to—."

"It's okay," he didn't let her finish. "But you do seem a little jumpy."

"My daughter has been taken is what is wrong with me."

"Don't you think you should call the police?"

"Will the police go to South America?"

"No, they wouldn't be able to help."

"The man in that car and his friends can. I have to persuade him. But he's very hard-headed. Remember we hired your agency because we didn't want to go to the police."

"I am as buttoned lipped as I can be," he said.

Cody turned right off of Roswell Road, and then two more right turns; then they were back on Roswell Road, going in the same direction.

"He knows we're following him, Mrs. Cobb."

"Good, maybe he'll stop."

He didn't stop. Not before he pulled into the parking lot of an apartment complex. They followed Cody into the lot and stopped thirty yards from where he parked.

"We'll sit here until he goes to his apartment," Laura said.

Cody got out of his car and without looking back, he headed up a walkway to a building. He put his hand in his pocket and pulled it back out before he reached the door. After a brief pause, he opened it and went inside. When the door closed, Laura's bodyguard pulled into a parking spot. Laura pulled in a deep breath and let it out as she reached for the door handle.

"Are you going in there, Mrs. Cobb?"

"Yes, I have to. He is the only person who can help me."

"I don't like this, but you seem determined."

"I am. He is not going to hurt me. The worst thing he can do is turn me down."

Laura sat with her hand on the handle for a few minutes. "It's now or never," she said, and she got out, closed the door and hurried up the same walkway to the same door Cody did, a moment before. Her mind was working overtime. Oh, God, what am I doing? What if he asks me to leave? He could make me go. Laura stopped halfway up the walkway. The man at the club said Cody ain't as nice as he is. He was nice enough the other times we spoke. I had to stand my ground with him. Dirty money he called it. He was right, but it's worse, its filthy money, and it came from the scum of the earth. It came from people who kill. Oh, God the poor couple and their son. He might not open the door. He has to answer because I won't take no for an answer. For Christ's sake, my daughter's life could rest in his hands.

Before Laura realized it, she was inches from the door. She stood there looking at it. Quickly, her hand went to the small button and pressed it. She heard the sound of the doorbell coming from inside and she jerked her hand back and waited. She didn't hear any footsteps inside. Her finger went to the button and pressed it again, more determined than ever. Answer the door you big damn... answer the door. Another press, the door opened before she could back her hand away.

"Mrs. Cobb, what took you so long to decide to come in?" Cody asked. "I almost went to bed."

"May I come in?" Laura asked. Cody moved to the side and motioned with his head. She stepped through the door and stopped. Cody stood with one hand on the door, looking at her. She looked at him, then around the room. It was neatly decorated with nice furniture. Not what she imagined a single man's apartment would look like. It had a woman's touch.

CHAPTER 18

"Nice place, Mr. Billings, it has a decorator's touch," she said, hoping to break the ice.

"Thank you. I had plenty of help with it." Cody moved the door, only to halt it before it touched her.

"Oh, sorry," she said, and moved in so he could close the door. "How long have you known we were following you?" she asked, feeling somewhat more at ease. *I'm in.*

"Ever since you and your bodyguard left the parking lot of the club," he told her, as the door closed.

She stiffened when she heard it latch. "He said you would see us."

"Why so nervous?" Cody asked and moved around to face her.

"I'm not used to following people around early in the morning. How did you know it was me?"

"You're very noticeable. You're an attractive woman, Mrs. Cobb. But I don't think you're here to be told how pretty you are. What is it you want?" His being firm and to the point made it easy for Laura.

She told him about Ashley and the phone call from Lesmeck.

"I think it's time you and your husband called the police. I don't see how I can help you."

"They're taking her out of the country. Isn't it what you and your friends do? You get people back, don't you?" Laura said.

"Yes, we do, but I explained our situation to you before. I'll give you the number for someone who can help you."

"I don't want a number. I need your help, Mr. Billings. Did you not understand what I said about my daughter?"

"Your husband's company is tainted and—."

"I know how you feel about our money." Laura held her hands out as though she were offering him something. "We didn't make all of it with those people. Please understand." Laura said, in tears now. "If it's not money, what do you want?"

"Nothing you could offer, Mrs. Cobb. So please—,"

"Nothing I could offer," Laura cut him off. She looked up at Cody. "How did you say you recognized me in the car tonight? I'm a pretty woman, aren't I." She moved out of the three-foot space they occupied. "You like me? She opened her long coat. "How do I look, Cody? Remember, I told you to call me by my first name. Because I like you, Cody." Laura let her coat drop to the floor. She stood there in her bikini panties and bra, exposed and offering herself for the first time to a man other than her husband. Her body was untouched by the years past her early twenties and had escaped any signs of bearing a child.

Cody stood, staring at Laura. Standing before him was one of the prettiest bodies he had ever seen, and it was all his for the taking. He could do anything with this Goddess standing almost naked in his room.

"What do you want me to do first?" Laura asked. It was obvious she was uncomfortable and inexperienced pleasing strange men. Cody crossed his arms and turned his head to a closed door.

"The bedroom, of course," said Laura. "You want me to go in there first, sure. Do we have to?" Laura said, nervously. Thinking it wouldn't be so bad if she didn't have to go into his bedroom. She took a step towards the bedroom door.

Still, Cody said nothing. He put his arm out stopping her.

What's he doing? He hasn't said a word. "What do you want me to do?" she said and reached behind her back to undo her bra. "Oh, of course, take this off."

"No, not, not first," Cody said, holding a hand up.

"Okay, what?" she put her hands on her hips and hooked her thumbs in the elastic in her panties.

He shook his head. "No." He walked over, picked her coat up and handed it to her. "The first thing I want you to do is to put your coat back on. What do you take me to be, Mrs. Cobb?"

She did as he asked. "I feel so ashamed, I am so sorry, Mr. Billings. I don't know what came over me. I don't know what to say."

"What, no more first names? Am I back to Mr. Billings now?"

"I'm not sure about anything anymore. I don't know my husband. I'm not sure I know who I am right now."

"I know who you're not. You're not the woman who was standing in front of me a few minutes ago,"

Cody assured her.

"That I'm sure of myself but that is all." The phone in another room rang.

"Please if you'll excuse me, I have to get it." He left her standing in the middle of the room.

A few minutes after Cody left for the other room, a tall blond came out of the bedroom wearing scanty panties held in place by curvy hips below a small waist. Her bra covered the bottom of her firm 'D' sized breasts. She walked sensuously into a kitchen not much bigger than a walk-in closet and opened the refrigerator, pulled out a container and filled two glasses, walked over to Laura with a glass in each hand. "Have some juice?"

"What is it?" Laura asked, still stunned by the presence of the woman and not wanting to look at her.

"It's papaya, pretty good without the disgusting brewer's yeast Cody puts in it. I could put some Vodka in it if you want me to," she said.

"I think I could use a drink."

"I'll make it weak." The blonde walked back to the kitchen and placed both glasses on the counter.

"Not too weak," Laura said.

"Sure, you probably need it." She picked up a bottle and poured some of the contents into one of the glasses, picked it up, walked back to Laura and stretched her arm out.

"Thank you," Laura said, took the glass and quickly took a hefty belt, handling it better than she had the night at the club.

The blonde bombshell with deep blue eyes stared at Laura. "I'm Tiffany," she said, her lips full, face heart shaped.

Laura took another sip from the glass. "My name is Laura."

"Laura Cobb," Tiffany said. She walked over and leaned on the bar, separating the living room from the kitchen, strands of long, silky hair fell in front of her shoulders and rested on her breasts. "Since it's panty and bra night at Cody's, I didn't think you would mind my getting into the competition." She sipped at the juice.

Laura took another drink from the glass. "I apologize. It was a foolish thing to do. I can explain." Laura was more embarrassed than she had been with Cody.

"No need to, I heard your story. When the doorbell rang, I listened. When I heard a female voice I looked, cracked the door, only a little. You could never buy Cody with that trick. Rather than tell you, it was best to show you why. I'll get dressed now. He's in the shower. He'll be back in a bit." When Tiffany got to the door, she turned and said to Laura, "You do have a nice body." She left the room to dress.

Tiffany came back stuffed into in a pair of white hip huggers jeans and a blue body shirt. She took a seat on a stool at the breakfast bar she had leaned on and brought her feet up and placed then on a metal ring at the bottom of the stool. "It's true what you said about your daughter, isn't it?"

"Yes, it is true. Do you think I would have disgraced myself if it wasn't? I have to convince Cody."

"He believes you, if not you would have been out the door by now. I know you're telling the truth. And it wasn't your stripping and offering yourself to

Cody. I am Dr. Bedot. I was on duty when you were brought to the hospital. I treated you and you kept saying something about having to find your daughter. Your husband said it was because of your fall. He wanted me to give you something to make you sleep through the night. He doesn't know I didn't. Needless to say, I was, I guess, shocked to see you turn up here almost naked in Cody's living room. I didn't mean it like you might think. But where are your clothes?"

"My husband was going to bring me a fresh change. He didn't count on me not sleeping until morning, I guess. I'm sure he didn't think I would take off into the night."

Cody emerged fresh from a shower. "I don't know why, but it seems as though your situation has gotten the attention of my friends," he told Laura.

"I don't understand."

"I know you don't. When I tell you what I'm talking about you'll have to go home, stay put and not communicate with anyone. Do I have your word?"

"Yes, I promise. Please tell me," Laura said, moving to the edge of the couch. "I'll do anything, I mean I *won't* do anything, talk to anyone, or go anywhere."

"I'll take you home. When we get outside, you'll tell your bodyguard."

"Does this mean you'll help me?" Laura asked Cody after they settled into his Mustang.

"I don't know what it means. All I know, for now, is someone has asked for a favor. When I mentioned you, he told me all he could on the phone, and I'll get more after I drop you off and meet my partners."

After a few miles, Laura touched Cody's arm. "Are you aware someone is following my bodyguard?"

"Yes, she would be Tiffany. She's a doctor."

"I know, she told me."

"She'll stay with you for a little while. Her idea, not mine, but I think it is a good one."

"She knows all about what you do?" Laura asked.

"No, not everything, but enough to know not to say anything."

"I'll stay in and not talk. You will do everything you can?"

Cody looked at Laura. "Everything," he said as they pulled into Laura's driveway.

"My husband's not here. I wonder where he could be. He's the cause of all this and he runs off and leaves me in the hospital."

After they entered the house, Cody asked, "Was it Lesmeck who called you about your daughter?"

"Yes."

"I'll need a picture of your daughter."

Laura walked to a table in the den, picked up a frame and struggled with it. "Take this one, it's from Christmas." She handed Cody a snapshot small enough to fit in his jacket pocket, which is where he put it after he glanced at it.

After a thorough check of the home's interior, Tiffany escorted him to the door. After giving her a brief peck on her lips, he left. He drove past the car with the guard sitting in it.

"Where is he going?" Laura asked Tiffany.

"To meet his friends is all I know. I don't know where."

Cody's partner was on the phone when he walked into the hangar at Fulton County Airport.

"All right, I got you. Sure enough, we'll find 'em and then we'll take hell to them." He hung up. "Cody."

"Major. Did you pick up anything about diamonds being moved through South America?" Cody asked.

"Yeah, I did, about a dozen groups move African glass in and out. Thing is, we don't know which one this family is mixed up with. I found out where Lesmeck lives."

"Let's armor up and go. How far?"

"Close to town, Fifth Street, and Durant Place. Better take my Buick, your car is a little loud to be running around town this time of morning."

Cody agreed.

CHAPTER 19

The men parked fifty feet up the street from Lesmeck's address, got out of the car and walked down the sidewalk to the house. They stopped and gave the area the once over before proceeding to the front door. James put a hand on the knob. The door was open about three inches. He looked at Cody and gave a gesture to enter. Inside the house was dark except for a ribbon of light shining through a slightly opened door down a hall.

"I'll go first," Cody whispered, and led them to the door the light was coming from. Cody peered inside the room and saw orange legs with a rope tied around them. They burst into with Cody rushing across the room and James going to his left. The legs belonged to a long, slim man wearing an orange suit.

Cody walked over and pulled a gag off the man's mouth. "Where's Lesmeck?"

The man frowned and looked away.

"Hey, Pumpkin Suit, I'm talking to you," Cody said. The man tightened his lips. Cody put a gun barrel to his head but still got nothing.

"I got this," James said, and got on one knee with a knife in one hand. "If you don't tell me where Lesmeck is I'm going to cut your clothes off and burn them. I have to tell you, I'm not very careful."

The man jerked back. "Please don't touch my suit. I'll tell you. A madman took him."

"Who took him? And what's your name?"

"Jay, my name's Jay. The Cobb fellow and an older man came bursting in like wild ass madmen, waving a gun, blew a damn hole in the wall, right up there."

They looked at the big hole in the sheetrock.

"Looks like a forty-five," Cody said. "Lucky it wasn't your head. Which is where my weapon will land if you don't tell us where they took Lesmeck."

"I don't know. He wanted some names from South America and Miami. The boss wouldn't give them to him, so they took him after the younger fellow tied me up. And I swear I don't know where they went. Cut my hands free, they're too tight, please." James cut the ropes, freeing his hands.

"What's in there?" Cody pointed to a door.

"Closet," Jay said as he pulled a knife and made a swipe at James, but he was slow. James wasn't and planted a big right fist to the side of his head and knocked him out cold.

Cody walked to the door and opened it. "We'll put him in here, then make a phone call," Cody said.

They tied him up, dragged him to the closet and tossed him in.

"Let's go, I saw a pay phone a few blocks away," James said.

Cody made a call. "Mrs. Cobb, this is Cody. I need the address of your husband's company."

"It's on Moreland Avenue, inside Interstate 285; Cobb Trucking is on the front of the building."

When they reached Cobb Trucking, they found the gate open. Major pulled through and stopped halfway down the parking lot. The building was a freight dock with a roof and no walls, just with spaces wide enough to park two trailers side by side at each door. You could see all the way through the building.

"Hold on. Roll down your window," Cody told James. "Do you hear something?"

"Yes, I do. Sounds like a diesel engine. It's on the other side of the building."

"Cut the lights and follow the sound," Cody said. Around the building in the middle of the lot were two tractor cabs without trailers, back-to-back. There was something connecting to the back of each truck like they were going to have a tug of war. They drove over for a closer look.

"I think I know what I'm seeing but I'm not sure." James said after they stopped.

"If you think it's a person connected to those trucks, it is. I think we have found Lesmeck."

"Damn right it is," said James. They got out of the car and walked closer to a man standing beside the truck who was busy attaching something to its frame.

James spoke out, "Mr. Cobb?" The man didn't respond. "Mr. Cobb." It was louder and followed with a tap on the shoulder.

The man jumped and whirled around. He was a lot older than who they were looking for.

"Are you Roy Cobb?"

"No. Who are y'all?"

A man came from around the truck with a gun pointed at them. "Who are you, and what do you want?" he demanded over the noise of the truck's engines.

"Are you Roy Cobb?" Cody asked.

"Who wants to know?" the man asked, then moved the gun chest high. He pointed it from one to the other a few times.

"Mr. Cobb, your wife came to see me," Cody told him. "She said your daughter was in trouble. I'm Cody Billings and this is—"

The older gentleman spoke up quickly. "I told you, Roy. It's them. I told you my friend was telling the truth. They are real and I knew it. Gentlemen, thank you for coming."

"And you are Mr. Windsor," James said.

The man snapped to attention. "Present, Bird Colonel Robert Windsor, retired," he said.

"I take it this fellow all tied up here is Lesmeck," Cody said, and examined the man held up by the chains connecting him to the two trucks. "What are you going to do?"

Roy walked over and switched off the truck's engine and walked back. "I'm going to get him to tell me who has my daughter and where she is."

"A very persuasive method, all right," James said.

"I'll tell you nothing. You, son-of- a-bitching madman, you damn fool," Lesmeck shouted.

"You two not going to stand there and let him do this to me, are you?"

"No, we're not," James said.

"See, I told you, Cobb, they are not going to stand there and be a witness to murder," said Lesmeck.

"And you're right. We are not going to stand here. We are going to move over there, so we won't get splattered with blood." Cody said. "Where do you think he'll come apart, James?"

"Kind of hard to say, I never saw a man pulled apart before, maybe the waist. I can't wait to see. Carry on, Mr. Cobb," said James.

"You can't mean that. You won't get away with this, none of you," Lesmeck yelled.

Roy got in one of the trucks, fired up the engine and revved the engine, then let off the fuel. When he pressed the clutch and put the transmission in gear, there was a forward movement. Everyone jumped.

Lesmeck began yelling over the noise of the diesel, "STOP, I'll TELL YOU. Please get me down from here." He was shouting out names and places so fast they couldn't understand him.

Robert Windsor ran to the front of the truck and threw up his arms. "Shut her down, Roy. He's singing like a bird," he shouted.

Roy cut the engine and jumped down. "I knew he would."

"I'll talk," Lesmeck cried. "His name is Fidel Lopez. I'll tell you everything. Please don't pull me apart, please."

"Let's hear it," Cody said. "All you can tell us. If you lie to us, we'll come back and tear you from limb to limb."

Lesmeck spilled the beans as fast as they could write. He gave them names in Miami and South America and the town, but he did not know the location where Ashley was being held.

"Our other team members should be at the airport by the time we get there. We'll be on our way south in about ninety minutes," James told them, then looked at Lesmeck, but spoke to Roy. "I'm calling some men out of North Georgia to hold onto this piece of garbage until we get back. Let's get him inside until they get here." They struggled to get the chains off Lesmeck, freeing him from his torture rack.

"Guys, I'm paying men to protect my family. One is at the hospital with my wife. The other one can keep an eye on this washed-up Al Capone," Roy told them.

"No, I'm sure those fellows are good." Cody said, and told him, "But we use our men, or we don't work. And your wife is not at the hospital. She's at home, and she's fine. There is a doctor with her."

"I'll pull a trailer out and put Lesmeck in it, then back it up to a pole so the door can't be opened. We'll wait for your men," Roy assured them.

"You can keep your men, Mr. Cobb, but we would appreciate it if you would welcome a couple of our men to stay at your home. You must do what I tell you no matter what. When our men get here, go home," James told Roy. He got no argument.

Back at the airport, one more call was made. "Mrs. Cobb, Cody again. Do you remember what you're to do until we get back?"

"Yes, I remember. Go nowhere, talk to no one. Correct?"

"The same goes for your husband. Make sure he understands. He'll be home soon with the company of two of our men. We're off." The connection was lost.

CHAPTER 20

South America

A few minutes after talking to Laura, Cody, James and their friends were in flight headed to Bogota, Columbia.

James gave them the information. "According to our source down here, there's a teenage American girl being held in a house on the edge of town. When we get there, we'll get a layout of the grounds. Best count our contact got, there's about six to eight gunmen in and out of the house."

"Wake me when we get there," Cody told them.

"Same for me," came from James.

The Cobb Home

"How long have you known Mr. Billings?" Laura asked Tiffany.

"Last Thanksgiving, I was working at a hospital in Honduras. Cody and his men brought an American man in. He was sick with a high fever when they rescued him from across the border in Nicaragua. He wouldn't have made it back in his condition. My work there was finished, and I was on my way out the door to catch a plane home as they were coming in. Because I stayed to treat him, I missed my plane, so they flew me home. They have a jet. Cody and I developed a relationship after that."

"Where is home?" Laura asked.

"Dallas, Texas."

"Did you make it home?"

"No, actually I was coming to Atlanta. I had thought about going home, but I had a job at the hospital where you were tonight. I will go back home someday, maybe soon, I don't know."

"What about Cody, will you leave him here or will he go with you?"

"Cody? No." Tiffany laughed. "Cody and I are, what can I say? Lovers, is what we are."

"Really, are you sure he feels the same way?" Have you asked him to go?"

"Give up what he does? Could you put a wild animal in a cage? Would you clip an eagle's wings?

"I don't know, I've never known a man like him," said Laura.

"There's not a lot of men like him floating around. He keeps me happy."

"My husband's not a wild animal nor does he have wings, but he does a very good job of keeping me happy."

"It's fine if a house and family is what you want."

"He can provide me with everything I need when I need it. I have no complaints, ever."

"I'm sorry. I should not have said what I said. You are quite a woman, Mrs. Cobb. If your husband can keep you happy, then he must be quite a man. I know I will never have Cody the way you have your husband."

"I wouldn't say it's only Cody. Besides, you wouldn't want him the way I have Roy; you said it."

"I think you're right. The adventure in him excites me."

"I can understand. My husband goes to the office every day and has his trucks move freight. Not very much adventure, I'll say."

"But you have what you want? I'll go to sleep now. If you have any pain or get dizzy wake me."

South America

"Rise and shine," pierced Cody's ears after he felt a hand on his shoulder, followed by, "Bogota, time to have some fun, men," came from Williams, one of the team's two pilots.

Cody sat up, rolled his head a few times and looked around. "Where's my steak and egg breakfast with coffee?" he asked.

"In your dreams, is where," Williams said.

"My dream is where I saw it," Cody said. "I guess James is out getting us all the information."

"Yea, he met our contact in town. He's back."

Cody took a glance out of the window. "Damn, Carlos is a good man. He's loyal and knows everything going on in this area."

"Yea, us getting his kid back from those rebels has sure paid off. You can't buy his kind of trust. See the small building over there next to the hangar? We are meeting the guys there and are having breakfast. I'm on my way. You coming?" Williams asked.

"Sit down, men. Let's go over what I have," James said. He reached his foot under the table to a chair across from him and pushed it out.

Cody turned the chair around and straddled it to sit down. "She must be the waitress. You want coffee, Williams?"

Williams pulled a chair from the table next to them, turned it same as Cody did and plopped down. "Affirmative. Black and no sugar."

"I have to have cream." Cody put a hand in the air. "Dos cafés con leche, por favor," he said.

A few minutes later the waitress placed two cups of coffee and a container of milk on the table.

"Pass me the sugar down here," Cody said to Charles.

The meal wasn't steak and eggs, but the men did enjoy it. After breakfast, they went back to the Learjet and took a nap.

The Cobb Home

"You're up, finally. I thought you would sleep all day, and I couldn't bring myself to wake you," Laura told Roy when he came into the kitchen.

"I was exhausted, but you know how I hate sleeping late." He rounded the table and took a seat.

"This is Dr. Tiffany Bedot. She's a friend of Cody Billings. She also works at the hospital."

"Yes, I know where she works. I met her last night. I had no Idea she was part of some commando rescue team," he said in a not so friendly tone.

"I'm not a member of any team. I happen to be an acquaintance.

"Well, what a coincidence the doctor who treated my wife knows the men who will save our daughter," he said in the same tone.

"Let's say it is a small world, Mr. Cobb."

"I also thought I asked you to give my wife something to make her sleep," Roy said. "However, if you had, I don't think those men would have believed my father-in-law. So, I guess I should thank you."

Laura picked up the coffee pot. "I think you owe Tiffany a big thank you. Had I been asleep I would have never gone out and found Cody." Laura said as she poured coffee into his cup.

"Well, Tiffany, tell me, did it take Laura's going to him to get the ball rolling?"

"All I know is, Cody told me his friend called and said he had gotten a call about your daughter, but he was going to dismiss it. Until Cody told him about Laura being at his place and he had spoken with her before. So, your wife is the one who deserves all the credit."

"Who are these men they sent to our home, Tiffany, do you know them?" Laura asked.

"I have only met them once. They live up in North Georgia on top of a mountain in a, uh, well, you would not believe it. Anyway, they will protect you."

"They seem so educated and well-mannered. Not what you would expect from someone who does what they do," said Laura.

"They all have college degrees," Tiffany said.

"Are those guys as good as we've heard?" Roy asked Tiffany.

"I only know about what they've done since I've known them, and what I've been told. They've never failed on a mission. Your child will come home. Laura tells me your daughter is very intelligent. It will help her get through this."

"She is, and she reminds us of it every day. What puzzles me is where she got it from."

"I'm sure both of you made contributions," Tiffany said.

Roy forced a slight smile, sat back, brought his cup to his lips and let his thoughts leave the ladies and find their daughter's first day of school.

'Well, good morning, who do we have here?' The teacher greeted them as they entered the classroom for Ashley's first day at school.

'My name is Ashley Windsor Cobb.'

'Ashley, would you please take a seat next to Julie? Raise your hand, Julie.'

A hand went up.

'Yes, ma'am, I sure will.' Ashley went to the empty desk. "Thank you, Julie, my name is Ashley, how are you this morning?' asked the precocious child.

CHAPTER 21

South America

Two hours before dark, the team packed themselves into a rental car and drove to the house Carlos had told them about.

"There it is up ahead. Pull over right here," Cody told the driver. "Pull behind that tall brush."

Williams stopped the car out of sight and the men exited. The house was surrounded by tall bushes, high enough to move around in without being seen.

"Not another house in sight. Better than we expected," Nicholas said.

"We can't leave any of those guys alive, can we?" Williams asked.

"Nope, if we do the Cobb family will always be in danger," Cody said.

"Those two on the porch, see what they're carrying?" Nicholas said. "We're up against some heavy firepower." He was referring to the AK-47s they'll have to face.

"Carlos said there are two honchos; one rides around in a big, black Cadillac," James said. "The other he said is not from this country. He has a Buick 225, white. Neither is here, so we'll have to wait till they get back. We want to take them all out in one scoop. If we go in now the others could come back in the middle of it. They'd scatter all over this town, making it impossible to find them."

After an hour of waiting the faint sound of an approaching automobile filled the air.

"Caddy coming, large and black, must be one of our guys," Charles, the explosives expert and muscle man said. "Yep, two scumbags inside," he said as the car turned into the driveway and stopped close to the house. The driver got out and took a long look around before he opened the back door. A short, slim man, wearing mirrored sunglasses stepped out. He looked around for a few seconds before he stepped away. When he did, his chest was pushed out and he held his arms out from his body a few inches. His steps were slow and stiff as if he were too big to move any faster.

"He's a little piece of crap with the short-man syndrome. I hate 'little' shits who act like they are bigger than everybody else." said Williams, who was twice the size of the man he was referring to.

"Another car coming, looks like a Deuce-and-a-quarter." James said. "That's it." They watched it drive by and turn into the driveway and stop next to the Cadillac. The passenger got the same service the man in the Caddy had gotten from his driver.

"Look at that. Do you guys recognize him? The son-of-a-bitch?" Cody asked them.

"Hell yes, I do," Nicholas said, followed by agreements from the others.

"Captain Dung Minh," James said. "I never thought I'd see 'hide nor hair' of him again. If ever I wanted to put a North Vietnam soldier in the ground, it was Captain Dung Minh."

"How many civilians do you think he killed doing his raids on those villages?" Williams asked.

James said, "Too damn many to think about is all I can say. It was his camp we raided the night we were betrayed. We lost our friend who would have been our sixth team member in that raid on him. Remember, Captain Dung Minh let us know he knew, too."

"Tonight, our friend will have his revenge," Cody let it be known. "I say to the one who gets him, let him know who is taking him out and who it's for. Make sure Fender's name is the last thing he sees. As soon as it gets dark, I'm going in closer. I want to get a look inside the house."

"Ah, sweet revenge, how I do love it," Williams said.

After returning from casing the grounds, Cody advised them, "Here's what we're facing. There are seven in the kitchen playing cards and imbibing liquor. The girl is in the far front room, and she appears to be okay. They have her tied to a bed. We move in when the moon is behind the clouds," Cody instructed them.

"Did you find anything I can put to use?" Charles asked.

Cody pointed. "There's a shed at the back of the house. It's full of explosives."

Charles rubbed his chin. "Sweet, sweet music to my ears. Our job just got easier. I'll turn the house into splinters, and the shed with it."

Twenty minutes passed and James looked toward the sky. "Only one thing left to do, let's get it done," They made their way to the house in stealth fashion, one to the front door and one to the back door. The other three went to a window each. Cody stopped at the window to the room the girl was being held in and peered through it. He saw the room was empty except for the hostage. After each man checked a room Cody stood in place while four of them went to a corner each. James signaled to one of the men with a red lens flashlight who did the same to another man until the light was seen by each man. With the red lens they went back to their entrance position and waited.

Their timing was so precise each man touched the floor inside the house at the same time. They met in a hallway running from the front to the back door. After a moment of silence, they moved toward the kitchen like a lion shadowing its prey. Then something happened they had not counted on. Light from outside filled the front rooms on both sides of the hallway. It was coming from an automobile pulling into the driveway. They heard the car door slam shut. Whoever got out left the lights on and was double-timing to the house. Cody and the team stood frozen, waiting for someone to come busting through the door. Before that happened, two men walked out of the kitchen and stared straight at the team.

"Trouble," one shouted.

The other one turned and looked at the other end of the hallway. "Here too," he bellowed out as he raised his AK-47. He was too slow. One of the team members put a round between his eyes. Charles fired and sank one into the other guy's chest. James turned and brought the driver down as he burst through the door, brandishing and wildly firing a large caliber pistol. Cody and two team members rushed into the kitchen.

"Hands up, high," Cody shouted in Spanish while moving his weapon up and down. There were five guys in the room. Two were the leaders. Two were large and three were small.

"Don't you even think about it, Scumbags," Nicholas yelled as two of the bad guys looked at their weapons. It was the two big guys. He smashed them in their faces with the stock of his M-16.

Charles eased out the back door and around to a front corner of the house. He took aim at the dead driver's car. Three shots from his M-16 took the windshield and driver's door glass out. Two more shots put the lights out. A quick inspection of the car showed it to be empty.

Everything was under control inside the house. The team had untied the girl and gave her instructions to stay in the room until they came for her.

James looked down at one of the men and said, "Well, what a surprise, Captain Dung Minh. You know I thought we had seen the last of you four years ago."

The small statuesque man looked confused, then smirked. "Am I supposed to know you?"

"Think back to a night in Vietnam, early 1971.

"They are lots of nights in a year. I can't say any one was more memorable than any other."

"Maybe not to you, but there was one we'll never forget," James said, and then reminded him, "On this particular night your camp was raided. Because someone we had depended on didn't show, your men took out eight of our men."

"There was a war going on, people get killed in wars, Major James. I no longer need to pretend I don't know who y'all are. Each of your pictures hung on my wall long enough for me to burn your faces into my memory," Minh told James.

Charles reminded him, "Your men took out a friend of ours." James took him by the collar, yanked him up and kept lifting, until his feet dangled six inches off the floor. "You taunted us about it. Remember?" James said with a stern voice and then shoved him back down so hard it crushed the chair. "Get another seat, you pig's ass, you," James said.

"Tell me something," the man said who came up in the Cadillac. "How did you men happen to find out about us and our location?"

"I guess I can tell you since you're not going anywhere. It was Lesmeck. He has plans to take over down here and cut you guys out," Cody told them in Spanish. "Yeah, he's going to cut you all out. He thinks you people are as dumb as hell."

"The double-crossing, son-of-a-beech. We'll see who is dumb." the man from the Cadillac said.

Charles, the explosives expert, shouldered his weapon. "I have some work to do. I'll leave this matter to you guys. You go with me," he said, and pointed to the smallest man sitting at the table.

"Me?" the man said, and pointed to himself

"Yep, you," Charles said, grabbed the man by the collar and jerked him up, so quick his feet left the floor. "Go ahead of me." When they got outside, Charles asked the man in Spanish, "Did you understand what my friend said about Lesmeck?"

The man answered him in Spanish, "Si, Senor."

"Speak English if you can, my friend," Charles told him.

"I think Lesmeck will be in a lot of trouble if we get out of here," the little man said in English.

Charles stopped at the shed and said to him, "These men I'm with are crazy, you know. They're going to kill everyone in the house. What would you think if I were to let you go?"

"Oh, Senor, I think yes, very good idea," he said, shaking his head up and down.

"Well, I tell you what. I don't like those men I'm with very much. But I like you, and I'm going to let you go right now, so take off. I'll tell them I killed you." Charles sent him on his way.

All the men in the room were bigger than Captain Dung Minh, even the man from the Cadillac. Cody looked at the two biggest Spanish men who were by all means very large. He pointed to one of the two.

"What's your name?

The man spat blood. "Pablo," he said. Cody pointed to the man beside Pablo.

"Ramon," he responded, after he spat a tooth out. and asked, "What is your name?"

"It's not important," Cody told him.

"I want to know the name of the men I'm going to kill," Ramon said.

"Well, the first thing you have to do is get out of here alive." Cody looked around. "Odds are not in your favor."

"We see about that, American man. We see who leaves here."

Cody stood over the man. "Oh, we are all going to leave here. But not all of us will leave alive."

CHAPTER 22

"It was you guys who went to the woman's home and tied her to the bed." Cody said.

Pablo gave his friend a bloody smile.

Ramon grinned, showing missing teeth and put his hands up and brought them down with a couple of in and out motions as though he was drawing a woman's shape. "So pretty lying there in her black panties and bra. I wanted so much to take them off. But the American would not let us. He was soft, like her body. Next time we finish the job."

"Maybe with the young one we have here," said Pablo. They both laughed.

"Don't count on there being a next time," Cody said in Spanish, and then switched back to English. "Hombres, you like to fight Americans.

"I like to fight Americans. I chew them up and spit them out," Pablo said.

Williams grinned. "Which one of you wants to take one of us on?"

"You have weapons. You will shoot us," Pablo protested.

Williams put his weapon down. "I'm unarmed, gentlemen. Who's first?" he said, then rubbed his hands together.

"Ha, I will take you on. If I can leave after I am

finished with you," said Ramon.

"It's a deal," Cody said.

"Then I will take one of you. We will both be free to go, Ramon," said Pablo.

For any other man in the room to take on any member of the team would have been like David taking on Goliath without a slingshot. But these two Spanish men were equal in size to the members of the team.

Ramon came up quickly with a fist aimed at Williams's right jaw. He missed and stumbled across the room. Williams kicked him in the butt, sending him crashing into the wall. Ramon turned around clumsy and caught Williams on the side of his left arm and sent him backwards. Williams put a foot back and stopped himself, then sent a straight punch to his opponent's face. Ramon blocked it and swung wide at Williams's jaw. Williams turned sideways, away from it, and with lighting speed sent his right foot airborne, crashing into Ramon's head, knocking him sideways. When he came back to face Williams, he was met with a solid punch to the face sending him to the floor, out cold. Pablo seized the opportunity and came out of his chair, grabbed Williams around the waist and charged him back against the wall, trying to crush his ribs. Pablo backed his shoulder up, then rammed it into Williams's mid-section four times. On the fifth time the pilot came down hard with a forearm, weakening Pablo's grip, then put his fists together and came down between Pablo's shoulders so hard it sent the big Spanish man to the floor face first. Ramon had made it to his feet and took Pablo's place. He pressed Williams to the wall with a shoulder to his mid-section. The powerful American reached down and put his arms around Ramon's waist and lifted him up until his feet were touching the ceiling and his back was to Williams's chest. Williams fell forward and landed on top of Ramon, crushing his belly on the floor. Both Spanish men had to be helped to their chairs.

With it all settled as to who was the greater of the men, the team tied them to all their chairs.

Charles came back inside. "All ready if y'all are," he said.

James turned to Dung Minh. "You will remember our friend's name before you die. Let's get the girl and get out of here."

They went outside and piled into the station wagon and headed down the road.

Back at the house, Dung managed to free himself. "Dumb, stupid Americans, I kicked their ass in my country, and I will do it here," he said as he untied everyone else. "Let's go, we mustn't let them get out of this country." They all headed to the front door. "Let me open it," said the Vietnamese. He jerked the door open and saw a note hanging on a string. "What the hell is this," he said, and read the note, "You killed me in Vietnam. You're dead, Sergeant Fender, US Army, friend of Major James and team." It was the last thing he saw before the house exploded.

Less than a half mile from the house, the team heard a loud, "BOOM." They looked back at the brightly lit sky behind them.

"Did y'all blow up the house?" Ashley asked.

"Let's say they had some good explosives in a shed, and I don't think they knew how to store them safely," said Charles.

"I guess it's a little late for them to learn now. Keep driving. We'll be at the airport in one hour," James said.

They were fifteen minutes from the demolished house.

"Hey, what's this, more bad guys," Cody said as a car pulled in front of them and stopped abruptly. He put a foot down hard on the brake pedal, but their station wagon hit the car and knocked it about thirty feet ahead of them.

"I got one ready," Williams said, and leaned out a window and tossed a grenade under the automobile as four men jumped out with weapons in their hands. The blast lifted the car upward as it sent the men in different directions. Cody and his team were on the ground with guns ready when the men got to their feet.

"All right, drop em," James yelled in Spanish, then fired over their heads. The men threw their weapon on the ground

The team crouched behind their vehicle when they saw a set of headlights pop into view. As the car approached, the rear window eased down, an arm came out, the hand waving a white cloth.

When it stopped beside them, a man's face emerged. "You will have to excuse my men they were trying to stop you so I could thank you for ridding me of some very troubling competition," he said. His English was good with only a hint of an accent to tell them he was from South America. "If you would permit me to leave my card," he said. He held a card between his fingers." Maybe you men could join me some time when you return to my country." He flicked the card onto the hood of their car. "I'll send someone for my men," he said as they drove off. When he reached the blown-up vehicle, he said, "Idiots."

"What did he say to those men?" Ashley asked.

"He told them how fortunate they were," Cody said, and reached for the paper on the hood. "Anybody got a light?"

"Right here." James pulled a small cylinder from his belt and pushed a button on the back of it sending out a beam. Cody held the card out.

James took it and held it under the light. "It says he's in the diamond and gem export business. Legally, I guess, and we got rid of some of his competition."

They looked at the crumpled front end of the station wagon.

"No steam coming from it or any other leaks. I guess it'll get us back to the airport. Load up, men," Cody said.

CHAPTER 23

Monday, March 17ᵗʰ 1975

"Mom, Dad, you should have heard it. The house blew up along with all the bad guys," Ashley said as Laura and Roy hugged their daughter. They were all so overcome with excitement, they didn't notice when the team and their friends left.

"So, how's Lesmeck enjoying North Georgia?" Cody asked his friend when they were in the car.

"He had a difficult time enjoying the scenery. I think he's more of a city boy," said their mountain friend. "As far as he knew, he was in North Carolina. He should be back in Atlanta before long.

"Time to hit the street," the driver said, and pulled the van over to the curb. "This is as far as we go."

One of the men got out and opened the sliding door. "Hop out," he said.

"Ah, come on, guys, it's four blocks to my house, you don't want me to walk, do you?" Lesmeck said.

"The walk will do you good. Oh, check your closet when you get there," one of the men said, as they drove off.

After a ten-minute walk home, then climbing eight steps from the sidewalk to his yard, Lesmeck stopped for a breather. He then made the fifteen feet to the six steps and up to his front porch where he took a five-minute break in a chair before going inside. He checked all the closets. When he got to the last one, there he saw Jay in his orange suit, lying on his back with his legs stretched up the wall. He had a piece of rope around his body holding his hands in place so he couldn't move.

"What the hell are you doing in there?"

"Oh, Boss, I thought I never would get out of here," Jay said as he swung his legs out the door and let them hit the floor. "It feels good to straighten out. Untie me, will you. Where have you been? Man, things got a little crazy after Cobb and the old fellow took you. Two other guys came looking for you. Big and mean, I guess you were lucky Cobb took you first."

"Ah, shut up, Jay. Lucky my ass" He got on his knees and untied Jay. "I'll tell you what, I'm lucky I'm not a foot taller right now."

"A foot taller, what'd you mean, by that?"

"Never mind, can you get on your feet?" Lesmeck asked as he pushed himself up from the floor.

Jay put his arms and legs in the air and started shaking them.

"Damn, Jay, what are you up to? You look like a dying cockroach." He jumped back from the jerking man.

"Circulation, Boss, got to get the blood flowing back through my body. I hope this suit ain't ruined."

"When you get through doing your Elvis impersonation, call Martin," Lesmeck said on his way out of the room.

Sunday, March 23rd 1975

It was ten in the evening when Lesmeck answered the knock on the door.

"Alfonso, do come in. What brings you to my neck of the woods?" Lesmeck backed away from the door and let Alfonso and his two henchmen in. He pointed at Jay and Martin who were standing in front of the sofa. "You remember my associates."

"Yes, the colorful suits man. How could I forget?" Alfonso referred to the red suit Jay was wearing. "I'll get to the point, Lesmeck."

"The point? What is the point you will get to?" Lesmeck asked.

Alfonso turned and looked at his men, then back. "I'm sure you have heard about what happened to our affiliates to the south."

"Why, no, I have not heard. Would you mind filling me in?"

"You mean our entire organization in South America has been wiped out and you have not heard about it?"

Lesmeck's mouth was frozen half open. He thought, those damn friends of Roy Cobb. His head moved side to side slowly.

"What is an affiliate?" Martin said.

"It's having something to do with people working together, I think," Jay said.

Martin smiled. "Well, they ain't it no more."

"You mean Fidel is…?"

Alfonso nodded. "There is more I'm sure you haven't heard about."

Lesmeck formed his mouth to say, "More." But no words came out.

"I'm afraid Milo Gulchie is out of the operation too—he and his meritless son which will be of no loss at all. Someone got to them last night while he was unlocking the door to his house. You have not heard anything about this?"

"We were out of town until earlier today," Lesmeck said.

"Out of town, you say. How convenient. Were you in New York by any chance?"

"Heavens no. We were in Nashville at the Grand Ole Opry."

"You were at the Grand Ole Opry? You expect me to believe you?"

Lesmeck pointed. "Jay likes it, and I promised him I would take a trip up there with him to attend the show.

"Yeah, it wasn't bad. It's on the radio you know," Martin said.

Alfonso turned and nodded to his men.

"What is the meaning of this? Put those weapons away." Lesmeck said.

"Here's the way I see it," Alfonso said. "You and I are the only ones still alive. I didn't kill those guys. So, you are the only one who had a reason. I'm still alive because I was out of town the last couple of nights, and you couldn't find me."

"I've never heard anything so ridiculous," Lesmeck said.

145

"Perhaps it is," Alfonso said, and told his men, "Bring them into the kitchen."

Within a few minutes, all three men sat naked in chairs, their hands tied, and mouths taped. One of Alfonso's men pulled out a cattle prod, stuck it to Lesmeck's face and pressed a button. He began to jerk.

"That was for Milo." Alfonso pointed to the fat man's chest. "This will be for Fidel. On second thought I never liked Fidel, so you will get a pass on him. Let's see, where next?" He pointed to the man's crotch. "That will be for Angelo."

When the wand touched Lesmeck's genitals, he began to move frantically and muttered through the tape.

"Hold on, I think he wants to say something. He probably wants to apologize." Alfonso pinched the corner of the tape with two fingers and yanked it off, causing Lesmeck to cry out. "What is it you want to say? Before you say anything, I'm telling you, begging will get you nowhere."

Lesmeck shook his head. "Not down there. Remember you said you didn't like Angelo. I heard you. Y'all heard him, right?"

"You're right about that; I never did like him. Actually, I found him rather annoying with his constant talking."

"That's right, he was always talking down to us because Milo ran things," Lesmeck reminded them.

"So, for putting only one bullet in him—I should give you a double dose, but you might be useful. Get your clothes on, but only you."

"I'm sure I will be, Alfonso." Lesmeck pulled his pants on. "What about Jay and Martin?"

sister?"

"No, I did not know that."

"That's because I never told you. No more about that for now. You did a good job getting the diamonds moved."

"I have a very convincing way of doing business. And I can continue to be effective."

"Moving what? We don't have a source for diamonds," Alfonso said.

"If Fidel could find someone, so could we. Partner," Lesmeck said.

"Perhaps, but first, I have business here." Alfonso looked at the man with the prod, then he nodded toward the two men in the chairs.

"You first, slim." The man poked Jay and pushed a button, causing him to spasm. The man continued shocking him all over his body for a few minutes before he passed out and fell on the floor. He set in on Martin and gave him the same treatment until he passed out. The men threw water on them bringing them around.

"Get dressed. We're going for a ride." Alfonso told them.

"Where are we going?" Lesmeck asked.

"There is some business we have to take care of."

147

CHAPTER 24

The men climbed into a long black limousine. It had two bench seats in the front and one in the rear and one bench seat along one side facing the double doors. In all, it would accommodate twelve passengers. Jay and Martin sat in the back, Alfonso and Lesmeck and one of the other guys sat on the seat along the wall. The man faced Jay and Martin with a gun on them. Alfonso and Lesmeck looked out the window. While one man drove. They were going east on Interstate 20 beyond the city limits of Atlanta for several miles before they exited. After a few turns, they stopped at a construction site.

"I had my men out scouting the entire day for a suitable location. Everyone out of the car," Alfonso ordered.

"What are you going to do with my associates?" Lesmeck asked.

"You will see."

"If you don't mind Alfonso, I'll wait here."

"Suit yourself, but I thought we were partners. Besides, don't you want to say farewell to your men?"

"I guess it would be fitting. I'm sure they would want me to be with them at their final moment."

One of Alfonso's men led the way. "Single file behind him." Jay, Martin and the guy who prodded them, and then Lesmeck, followed by Alfonso.

Lesmeck said, "Fidel and his men were pigs when it came to women. You called him names for that."

"Yes, I did." Alfonso looked at the stars for a moment. "My sister was raped by two men like Fidel's men. And your men raped the Ludlow woman while her husband listened helplessly."

"I'm sorry for that, really I am, and Fidel deserved to die and his men, too," Lesmeck said.

"I feel the same as you about that."

"My sister couldn't live with what those men did to her, so one night she took the gun I had given her for protection, and she blew her brains out."

"I am so sorry to hear that," Lesmeck said.

"Yes, so was I." Alfonso slowly raised his gun and pointed it at the back of Lesmeck's head. "You called Fidel names, but you did nothing to stop your men from doing the same thing. I despise men who do that to women and a man who would allow such a thing." They stopped at the edge of a cluster of trees.

Tuesday, March 25th 1975

After returning from another rescue mission the previous day, Cody and his team members were at the apartment in Atlanta. The team had rented it for their out-of-town members to use when they were in town overnight. The team used it when they wanted to get together to discuss business. They invited their friends from North Georgia so they could fill them in.

Charles gave them a rundown. "The fellow I let go should have already contacted the men in Miami. I would say by now Lesmeck is in no position to bother anyone else."

"We'll have to take care of those boys in Florida," said James.

"Got a plan for that, Major?" Cody asked.

"Yea, I do, and the best thing about the plan is that we don't have to do anything," James told them.

"Well, what is it?" Charles asked anxiously.

"Do you guys remember the card that was passed to us on the road?"

"Sure, the man was in the diamond and gem export business," Cody said.

James walked around and leaned on the open bar that separated the kitchen from the living room. "I called Carlos and got him to do some checking around. It turns out this guy is very big in the business and the guys we took out had been taking a sizable chunk of that business away from him."

"It seems like we did a bigger favor for him than we thought," Charles said.

"Yes, we did," James said. "And not only were they cutting into his business by exporting hot stuff they were threatening his customers and their family members in his country." James went on. "It appears that we wiped out his entire crew, with the exception of the one we freed. With no one down there to handle things, the ring leaders will have to return to South America to recruit others. When they return, they'll be dealt with."

Wednesday, March 26th 1975

Cody sat down to relax. It had been nine days since the team returned Cobb's daughter back to them. To Cody and the rest of the team that mission was history. They didn't think much about their past missions. He pulled out the 'on' knob of his new, Admiral 25-inch color console television for which he had paid seven hundred and ten dollars. He took a seat on the sofa next to Tiffany. The screen lit up and the news came on.

"This in moments ago; three bodies were discovered in a wooded area east of Atlanta. They were hidden under some brush and would have gone undetected if not for a brightly colored suit on one of the bodies. Channel 5 interviewed the man who made the discovery.

What appeared to be a homeless man came on the screen. "I was walking along the road minding my own business and I spotted something red in the bushes. If he hadn't been wearing that red suit, I never would have seen them," the man said.

The anchor newsman came back on. "More on that story as it develops. We'll be right back after this."

The phone rang. Tiffany picked it up. "Hello." She paused, then said, "Yes James, he is right here." She passed the receiver to Cody.

"Major, what's going on?"

"I spoke with Carlos, and he said we should visit his country more often. People like it so much they find it difficult to leave. He told me that three men from Miami came down, and they won't be

151

returning." James hung up.

CHAPTER 25

Thursday, April, 10th 1975

When Roy answered the knock, he saw two men in suits, one taller than the other, both clean shaven, neat haircuts and displaying badges.

"Are you Roy Cobb, owner of Cobb Transport?" the taller one asked.

"Well, yes I am, what can I do for you?"

"Laura appeared at Roy's side. "What's going on, Roy?" she said her eyes fixed on the two metal shields.

"This is my wife, Laura," Roy said.

"The taller one spoke again. "Mrs. Cobb." Then he looked back at Roy. I'm detective Gretchen this is detective Hill. We'd like to speak with you."

"Sure." Roy looked at Laura, then back. "Is there something wrong?"

"May we come in, please?"

"Yes, please do," Roy said. He and Laura stepped to the side.

"Could I get y'all some coffee?" Laura asked.

Both men declined by shaking their heads. Then they looked around as though the conversation may be determined by the contents of the house.

After a moment, Roy said, "You wanted to speak to me about something?"

"Yes." Gretchen pulled a piece of paper from his pocket. "We found this freight bill in the home of a man who was killed a few days ago." He handed it to Roy.

Roy studied the paper longer than needed. "Yes, that's from one of my Miami shipments."

"Can you tell us what exactly the freight was? The bill says it was cement statues."

"Sure. Flamingos."

"Flamingos? Like the bird, that walks on long legs?"

"That's the only kind I know of," Roy said.

Gretchen spoke up. "I'll get to the reason we're here. A few weeks back Robert and Jennie Ludlow were murdered in their home. A couple of weeks ago three men were found dead on the side of the road in Lithonia out in DeKalb County."

"We heard about both of those incidents. They were terrible," Roy said.

Gretchen studied Roy's face. "Yes, they were. The reason we're here is one of the men from the side of the road had the couple's phone number in a book we found in his house. Your number was in it, too. He also had this freight bill in the same drawer the book was in. It's probably nothing, but we're checking with folks who had any contact with him."

"The customer would pick the freight up in a rental truck. I guess he had my number so he could call and see if the freight was there before he came over."

"He had your home number, Mr. Cobb. Why

did he have your home number?"

"That's not unusual; we're a small company. My dock foreman and I trade off handling problems that might come up after hours. I gave that customer my home number because he wanted to pick up his shipments on the weekend sometimes."

"This man was a known criminal. He was a diamond smuggler," Gretchen said. "We found airline ticket stubs in the home of that couple. They were for flights to New York and back. This Lesmeck was one the men left on the side of the road. He had associates in New York. It appears that Mr. and Mrs. Ludlow were working with them. We spoke to both of Ludlow's families, and they couldn't help us any. They were shocked to think that they would do anything like that. It wouldn't be the first time a good man and his wife went to the bad side to make a few bucks. Things are, they don't think about the impact it has on their family members. Their kid's going to make it, but he has to grow up knowing his parents were criminals."

Roy looked at Laura, then at both detectives. "No, he doesn't. They were decent people. Sit down I have something to tell you. Tell me first, how did Lesmeck go?"

"You sure you want your wife to hear this?" Gretchen said.

Laura spoke, "If you gentlemen will excuse me, I have something to do." She left the room.

"Well, did Lesmeck suffer very much?" Roy asked.

"I don't know how much suffering a man can do after he has the top half of his face blown off from a bullet that came from the back of his head."

EPILOGUE

Friday, May 3rd 1975

Cody saw her when she walked through the door. After a greeting from Harold, she walked to the back of the room where Cody stood.

"Mr. Billings, do you have a few minutes?" Laura asked him.

"I can't say I'm busy," he grinned.

Laura shook her head. "Not this time."

"Outside will be quieter." They went out front to the right corner of the building. "Now, what can I do for you, Mrs. Cobb?"

"You and your friends left without letting us thank all of you. One of the two things I want to do is thank you for bringing Ashley home safely," she said.

"Glad we could help. After all, it's what we do."

"And do well, too."

"The last time we spoke you said you blamed your husband for everything that had happened, Tiffany said the same thing. How are you handling that?"

"Things are better. He did clear that couple's name, so their son and families now know they were victims and not criminals. I was glad he did that. I realize now he was a victim too. He is a good person.

That's why I fell in love with him. He's an excellent father, too."

"Are you guys clear with the legal issues?"

"With Lesmeck's history of conning people into doing his dirty work and killing that couple. They said that he had killed another couple. And those men taking Ashley, they figured we had no choice but to go along with them. Oh, they tried to check on your team to make sure we were telling the truth. All anyone in Washington would do was confirm that a child was kidnapped and that she was rescued. I told them that a man came to me and said that he could get her back. Case closed.

"You said thanking me was one of the things. What is the other?" Cody asked.

Laura paused for a moment. "The other has to do with the night I came to your apartment. I'm sure you remember what I did."

"Cody smiled. "How could I forget?"

"That's what I'd like for you to do."

"You mean wipe it from my mind?"

"Look I want you to know I wasn't myself that night. I was under a lot of stress; I had bumped my head, and I did something totally out of character for me. I hope you know that."

"You don't have to explain anything. I know you weren't yourself."

"Well, you know how things get started." She hesitated. "What I'm trying to say is. I know how men like to talk. I'd really appreciate it if you wouldn't say anything about the way I behaved that night."

"You mean I'm supposed to keep it a secret that a gorgeous looking woman came to my apartment and offered herself to me. No bragging at all?"

"Mr. Billings, your humor is amusing. But I have a family, and I own a business. You know what I'm trying to say."

"Yes, I do. Let me explain something. No one would believe me anyway," Cody said.

"You mean no one would believe a woman came to your place and did what I did?" Laura said.

"Well, they might believe you did what you did. But they would never believe that I turned you down. And I can't lie about it. So, I'll keep it between you and me. How's that."

Laura smiled. "Okay," she said, and turned to leave.

"Oh," Cody said.

Laura turned to look at him.

"You do have a great body."

Laura looked around, then back at Cody. "Thank you," she said, and left.

The End